Returning Eden

Maria Mellins

CROOKED
CAT

First Purple Line Edition
Crooked Cat Publishing Ltd. 2016

Discover us online:
www.crookedcatpublishing.com

Join us on facebook:
www.facebook.com/crookedcatpublishing

*Tweet a photo of yourself holding
this book to @crookedcatbooks
and something nice will happen.*

For Mike, Dylan and Ezra

Acknowledgements

There are so many people to thank for their kindness, support and creativity over the course of writing *Returning Eden*. With gratitude I would like to thank the following:

My wonderful publisher and editors at Crooked Cat who made this possible, I am very grateful.

To Vicky at Midlands Storm Chasers, whose notes on extreme weather were invaluable.

The staff and students at St Mary's University, especially Lee Brooks, Jon Hackett, Richard Mills, Carole Murphy, Allyson Purcell-Davis, Damian O'Byrne and Daragh Minogue. Thank you for allowing me the time to complete *Returning Eden* and for fostering such a warm, creative and nurturing environment.

To my Mum, for her constant support and enthusiasm and for showing me what fun writing can be.

To my Dad, whose stories about the bad guys when I was little certainly caught my imagination.

To my sisters, whose knowledge of YA fiction and reader insights were so helpful.

To the rest of my family and friends for listening to me witter on about horror stories, monsters and goodness knows what else. I would like to mention Dave Shanks, the Walsh family, Tara Coppinger and Darren Mulryan in particular.

And finally, to Mike, Dylan and Ezra, the people I tormented the most with my incessant questions, drafts, redrafts and general one track mind, thank you for putting up with me and for inspiring me every day.

About the Author

Maria is a Senior Lecturer and researcher in Film and Screen Media at St Mary's University where she teaches modules on horror film, gothic fashion and screenwriting. Maria's fascination with horror and dark fairy tales began in childhood, she grew up reading Point Horror novels and watching as many scary movies as she could sneak past her parents. This interest quickly transformed into a career as Maria completed a PhD and published a book entitled *Vampire Culture*.

Maria has now written her debut novel *Returning Eden* and is very excited to continue with the series.

When not writing, Maria can be found playing with her two sons Dylan and Ezra.

Returning Eden

Prologue

Black ripples of water slithered up the beach. The sand was almost entirely consumed. Her green eyes fixed on a tiny crab that lay on its back; its legs frantically tickled the sky. She daren't avert her eyes, not even for a moment. She feared that a blink, a slight head movement, would make the pain too much to bear. She had to channel all of her energy into watching the creature; it was the only power she could reclaim.

She lay there and waited, and then the agony came for one last time. It pulsed through her, a slow dark hum at first, which deepened until it swallowed her whole. She writhed around in a body that was no longer her own.

And then... it was over.

She wiped a sodden strand of long dark hair from her cheek as she scooped up the tiny child. She didn't expect its skin to be so tinged with blue, but its eyes were full of life. She gazed into them and for a moment deluded herself that today was the first day of her new life.

The life she wanted.

She vowed that she would change everything, right every wrong, and there were many, if she could only keep her baby.

But it was already too late.

As the child cleared its lungs for the first time, it betrayed their position. She pulled the child in close; the water crept up around them. She clenched her eyes shut as the tears came, her arms clamped around the fragile little body that snuggled against her, for one last moment. The last moment she would ever have any semblance of good, of humanity.

Then they were on top of her.

They peeled back her arms as she fought with everything she had. The veins in her neck bulged, her teeth ground together, she let out a guttural scream. She kicked, bit, punched, scratched but in the end it was no use. There were too many of them and they were too strong. They ripped the child from her grasp and left her body to fall away like a soggy ragdoll.

Her tear-drenched eyes fell to the tiny crab. Its legs wriggled no more.

In that moment she made a vow that would define the rest of her existence. No matter what consequences befell her, one day, her baby daughter would be returned.

DARKNESS

Chapter One

Eden Hollow watched the undergrowth. Beads of sweat formed on her muddy forehead. The landscape was still and quiet, tranquil even, but she knew he was out there, biding his time. Just moments before, the dark towering figure with those strange, chilling eyes had been hunting her. In order to evade him, Eden must move now. If only she could get across the field to the house and find freedom. Flopping onto her belly, Eden crawled army style across the sodden, filthy ground. This was the riskiest part; devoid of shelter, with only long grass to conceal her, Eden's elbows dug deep in the dirt as she hurled her body across the last few feet.

But it had all been for nothing.

Eden stared down the barrel of a gun. The finger that clutched its trigger was dirty and pruned, and desperately needed a nail clipping. The finger squeezed and wet slimy water shot her at point-blank range in the head.

"You are it!" Dylan Blake looked triumphant as he pulled off his swimming goggles. He wore a cardboard box around his middle, ingeniously tailored to fit his small, four-foot frame. His legs were clad in a pair of his mother's red tights; his little sister's sick-stained muslin cloth was tied around his neck like a cape. He reached out and pulled a very wet Eden to her tiny feet. She was wearing a black wetsuit.

"Thanks for that. I'm pretty sure that you cheated, but I guess you had to win eventually." Eden flicked her brown birds nest hair away from her eyes. In one perfect movement she kicked the garden hose into her hand, turning the nozzle to release a water stream which sent Dylan flying back into the paddling pool. Everything was, once again, right with the universe. As usual, Eden had emerged victorious. Dylan had emerged with his tail between his legs only, this time, it was quite literally the case. Dylan took Eden's outstretched hand and slopped sheepishly into the house. His cardboard box was sodden and misshapen; it hung down from his waist like a tail, trailing the floor behind him.

Eden and Dylan spent most summer evenings inventing similar scenarios. In one form or another they would inevitably end up covered in dirt and water. Their parents called them inseparable and, in a way, they were, although it would be difficult to find two children that were more different, even at the young age of seven.

Dylan, despite his strong and much taller than average build, was a shy boy. He was inherently kind and cared for Eden in a way that touched all those who witnessed it. They had been friends since they were eighteen months old, when Dylan's mother Judy began child-minding for the Hollows. Dylan was not particularly taken with other children his age, but Eden was different. When they first became friends he used to brush her hair and pick her daisies from the garden. He would present her with the flowers so proudly, until he opened his clenched fist to see the flower buds were all squashed and withered. This didn't faze Eden. She just shoved them in her hair and went looking for the next obstacle to climb, or small space to crawl into, followed, as always, by Dylan.

Eden by comparison was tiny. She was naturally petite and doll like, with green eyes, dark olive skin, and mounds of long chestnut hair. She was created to be a princess, but disguised herself well as an urchin. All of her clothes were covered in holes, frayed on tree stumps and fences. She was strong spirited and knew her own mind. She would spend hours in Dylan's garden digging up ants, worms, earwigs, and spiders, whilst Dylan put Judy's Tupperware to good use, constructing safe, warm homes for the creatures.

As the pair grew older they began to walk to school

together with Judy in tow. One sunny Monday in July Dylan arrived at Eden's front gate. It was just before Eden's eleventh birthday and the start of the school holidays, which they had spent the best part of the year planning.

Dylan felt the familiar blend of excitement and fear as he edged towards the doorstep of Holly Cottage. Whilst he loved visiting Eden, Dylan always felt uneasy about her home. With an outstretched hand, Dylan batted away silky cobwebs that shrouded the entrance and glanced over his shoulder to see a tiny mouse scuttle from the undergrowth.

The cottage was a double-fronted white stone building with black window frames and ivy creeping across the walls. Its gardens were so overgrown that it looked more like the Amazon jungle than a little English village. But Holly Cottage did have two redeeming qualities. For one thing, it contained Eden, and for another, the backyard was positioned at the edge of Willow Woods. In the summer, Dylan and Eden would spend many afternoons there, skipping stones on the lake, pushing each other off the rope swing, and making hammocks out of the Weeping Willow tree branches.

On this Monday, Holly Cottage was absolutely silent. Dylan lifted the large iron knocker and banged as hard as he could. The noise resounded throughout the house, but no one came to the door.

Dylan tried once again. He remembered how Eden would usually bounce to the door, shirt hanging out and uniform crumpled. He longed to see that scarecrow-like girl appear in the doorway but instead it remained empty. Dylan returned again on Tuesday, and again on Wednesday, but still no sign of Eden.

Finally, after an entire month of persistence, Dylan accepted that there was never going to be an answer. Dylan walked through Holly Cottage's side gate, into the backyard, and made his way to the woods. He sat down in their usual spot by the lake and bowed his head. On the ground lay a collection of withered dead daisies. *But where was Eden?*

Chapter Two
Present Day

"Die. Go on. Die. Why won't you just DIE!?" Seventeen-year-old Liam Scott threw down the game controller in his usual slapdash manner. He winced as he looked up to see Dylan's disgruntled expression.

"Mate, seriously. Mum will kill me if we break another controller."

"Oops sorry, I just get so frustrated with this crappy game. I'll talk to Boobs, I mean Judes, and tell her I will make it up to her... however she likes."

"Seriously, Scotty, that's my mum. Are there no boundaries? And while we are on the subject of boundaries, that's my T-shirt you have on."

Scotty quickly removed Dylan's black Ramones T-shirt and threw it across the room, leaving him bare-chested in his low-slung jeans. Scotty was thick-set, well over six feet, and his family's Scandinavian heritage was clearly demonstrated by his blonde hair and blue glacier eyes. He was an impressive creation, but he knew it.

Dylan rolled his eyes at his friend's ridiculous gesture and continued to play the videogame.

"And by the looks of it, those are my boxer shorts too! I wouldn't mind, but are you really stooping as low as to steal the only boxers I can't even bring myself to wear?"

Scotty scowled at Dylan and jokingly stroked the waistband of his Kermit the Frog 'green love machine' boxers.

"Sorry Dyls, I forgot mine after football yesterday. I didn't think you would mind."

Amused that Scotty had just unwittingly declared that he had been wearing the same underwear for at least two days, Dylan threw the T-shirt back to Scotty and changed the subject to their usual topic – sport. Dylan and Scotty had been best friends since secondary school. They had both recently enrolled at Cantillon College for a further two years of study, before they had to think about applying to University, and deal with the prospect of going their separate ways.

The boys had shared a great deal over the years. Most recently Scotty had provided Dylan with a welcome distraction away from his parents' divorce. Dylan loved the fact that Scotty didn't probe, didn't try and comfort, but just somehow silently acknowledged the difficult time that Dylan was going through and presented him with an array of distractions. For that, Dylan would always be grateful. Of course he could never bring himself to tell Scotty how he felt, and contribute to that ever increasing head size of his, but deep down he hoped that Scotty knew.

Two hours later, after an epic session on Dylan's football game, Dylan and Scotty went downstairs for a snack. Much to Dylan's dismay, the conservatory doors were open, and his mother and grandmother were sunbathing in the garden.

"Oh here we go," Dylan muttered under his breath. It was unusually hot for September, and both Judy and Enid were wearing bathing suits, with cucumbers over their eyes; their feet were dangling in a paddling pool. Despite the heat, Enid dunked a Digestive biscuit in her cup of tea. Scotty eyed the pair and couldn't help himself; his natural cheekiness was difficult to keep at bay.

"Cor Blimey, it's like the Playboy Mansion out here".

The scene was, of course, anything but the Playboy Mansion. Judy and Enid had a collective age of one hundred and twelve, and their *Marks and Spencer*'s mature range swimming costumes certainly wouldn't be the natural attire of a Playboy Bunny. The women laughed at Scotty as they always did; parents loved Scotty.

Dylan didn't look up from making their sandwiches.

"We are off to Cantillon tonight, Mum. There's a fancy

dress Sixth Form ball, so we'll get the last ferry crossing back at midnight. Scotty might as well stay here, if that's alright?" Scotty practically lived at Dylan's house anyway.

"Of course Lovey, be careful on the water that late," Judy removed the cucumber from her eyes and looked at Dylan, "especially if you insist on sneaking some drink in."

"Nothing gets past you, does it Mrs B? All that Miss Marple must be rubbing off!" Scotty winked as he took a huge bite of his sandwich.

"You just remember that, Liam Scott. And speaking of being careful, if there are any nice girls there tonight, please make sure you..."

"Oh Jesus, DO NOT finish that sentence, Mum," Dylan turned as crimson as Enid's sunburnt legs.

"Time to go I think, Scotty. We have some costumes to make." Dylan ushered his grinning friend back into the house, whilst Judy was mid-sentence. Scotty lunged into the cupboard and grabbed some crisps before Dylan practically pushed him up the stairs.

Now, they would have to settle down to their main task of the day; making a costume for 'Living Dead' Ball. They had left everything to the last minute as usual.

Chapter Three

Sixteen year old Eden Hollow took a deep breath as she looked out across the water. It was early evening, her favourite time of day. It smelled like summer, the blend of cut grass, barbecues, and suntan lotion. Eden walked to the front of the five o'clock ferry to get a better view of the island. The seagulls screeched and soared overhead, a huge stone building loomed in the distance; Eden's tummy turned over.

Cantillon Island was both as impressive and as sinister as she remembered from her day trips as a child. In the centre of the island was Cantillon College. The college had been built during the gothic revival in the eighteenth century; it was dark grey in colour, with stained glass arched windows, and a south easterly tower, which gave the overall effect of a miniature castle. The college grounds oozed over the entire island. There was only a very small area of land that it didn't dominate and that was taken up by jagged shorelines, public gardens and a small cemetery. The vista reminded Eden of the famous offshore prison in America - Alcatraz.

The majority of college students lived with their parents in mainland Skull, a sleepy fishing village in South West England. Eden had grown up in the village, before her parents had moved abruptly to Worcestershire when she was eleven years old. Her parents had pleaded with her not to return, but this was the only place that had ever felt like home. Ever since *that stormy night* five years ago when everything had changed, Eden felt as though she was just passing time. She so desperately wanted to return, and come back to her childhood home, Holly Cottage, come back to her beautiful, but unsettling Cantillon and, most of all, come back to him.

The ferry docked and Eden made her way out of the harbour. She walked through the old cemetery, up a stone staircase, and under a grand archway that led to Cantillon College, where she had made arrangements to board.

The estate was so vast, it sucked her in.

A carnival had come to Cantillon for the duration of Sixth Former's 'Welcome Week'. Eden watched as a masked woman dressed in a silver sequinned leotard rode a white horse with pink and blue geranium flowers intricately weaved into its mane. Across the way two workmen erected a sign that read 'The Carnival Noir,' its bright lights and flimsy sets looked out of place amongst the historical grandeur of the island.

Eden was desperate to explore, but she was feeling exhausted from her long journey, so set about finding her room and fitting in a power nap.

Eden's dormitory was situated in Crookhaven Halls, one of three buildings which made up Cantillon's Halls of Residence. The magnolia rooms were very basic but a generous size, with two single beds, a kitchenette, and a small ensuite bathroom. The starkness of Eden's new surroundings paled into insignificance when she looked out of the large cathedral style window and saw the humbling view of the raging ocean. She watched the waves as they frothed and splattered. Then something strange caught her eye.

Eden felt a chill run down her spine. For a split-second, Eden could have sworn that she saw something emerge from under the waves. *Was it a fin?* It could have been a dolphin or a whale's tail that thrashed about as it dived under the surface, but there was something unsettling about the way it moved. It seemed to be more menacing somehow. If Eden didn't know better, she could have sworn that it slithered.

Then, it emerged again. But this time, Eden's blood

turned cold.

She saw it more closely now. It looked like an enormous black dorsal fin.

Protruding from under the frothy water, as if it was being carried in the mouth of the beast, was a human arm.

Eden blinked her eyes shut in disbelief. When Eden opened them, the abhorrent scene had completely disappeared. The water was calm and there was no trace of the creature or its victim. *Could she have imagined the whole grisly incident?* She was exhausted from her long journey and this wouldn't be the first time her vivid imagination had played tricks on her. Eden fixed her eyes on the sea and waited, but the ocean kept its beasts at bay once more.

"Get a hold of yourself girl, for God's sake," Eden said aloud. "Let's just put this one down to way too much caffeine and way too little sleep. It's not like anyone will believe you anyway. Toning down the crazy is definitely a good plan right now. Being the new girl will be hard enough, without adding tall tales of aquatic monsters to the mix."

Eden reached up to draw the curtains when she caught sight of a low grey cloud that bled into the blue sky. A solitary drop of rain splashed onto the window pane; a storm was coming. Eden had always loved storms. When she was a child, she would climb out of her bedroom window and sit on her roof in the pouring rain, watching as the lightning bolts darted through the sky.

Eden remembered the cold lonely winters back in Worcestershire. When Eden had begrudgingly arrived at her new home, she didn't know a soul. So in the absence of making new friends, Eden had opted to spend her time storm chasing. Aided by her bicycle and the radar imagery on the iPad that her father had bought for her birthday, Eden joined an online community of weather watchers, and began to photograph extreme weather. Her mother hated her new found hobby, but her father would occasionally give in to her pleas, driving her around the local area, chasing storms in their Land Rover. By the end of the year, Eden was determined to have her own driving license so she could photograph extreme skyscapes all over the country at a moment's notice.

Eden picked up her suitcase and placed it carefully on the bed. She unfastened the zip and pulled out a small weather station from the otherwise modestly packed bag. Ordinarily Eden would prefer to use more basic homemade weather kits. She thought there was something more satisfying about working with standard thermometers, barometers, wind vanes and rain gauges. But dredging equipment around was difficult, so she had invested in a new combined digital version. She glanced around to check that the coast was clear, as she didn't want her new roommate to think she was a complete geek before she had even had a chance to get to know her. The room was silent, so Eden opened the window and carefully set about attaching the weather station to the outside wall.

It took some time to make sure it was correctly positioned, but once she was satisfied, she unpacked the remainder of her suitcase and then tucked herself under the covers. She felt the warm snugly glow that only a day-sleep could bring. The last rays of sunshine gleamed through the window and warmed her face, the sheets smelled of lavender. She drifted off to the sound of the waves crashing against the rocky shoreline.

Her sighting of the dark shadow lurking under the ocean's surface still preyed on her mind.

Eden's sleep was filled with broken dreams. A montage of abstract images flicked through her mind like the frames of an old movie.

Snakes were curling around trees in a forest. They slithered towards her, hissing and spitting venom. They exposed their fangs, she was paralysed.

She tried so hard to move her legs, to run, but it was no use.

Her toes crumbled to black ash, then her shins. The

diseased flesh spread slowly up her body, until there was nothing left.

Eden woke with a start. Her eyes flew open as she looked down at her body. She was relieved to find all her limbs intact, but was rather startled to see a girl sitting at the end of her bed. For a moment she thought she was still dreaming. She sat up, rubbed her eyes and smiled hesitantly at the fiery-haired stranger.

Niamh Finnerty was sprawled casually at the end of Eden's bed, clad in a navy dressing gown and ridiculous cow print slippers; she was reading a celebrity magazine. Noticing that Eden was awake, she craned her neck and peered around the glossy pages.

"Now then, I have run you a bath and made you a nice cuppa tea. Sorry to wake you, but I didn't want you sleeping through the Sixth Form Ball tonight. If you're anything like me, you'll need hours to get ready." Her thick Irish accent practically sang the words.

Eden just stared at her as she tried to come to. She was struggling to lift her sleep hangover and Niamh seemed like a whirlwind of energy by comparison. Niamh passed Eden her tea and popped a biscuit in her hand.

"There you are. Oh, sorry. I'm Niamh Finnerty by the way."

Despite her own grogginess, Eden suspected that she was going to like Niamh. She was pretty, in a different sort of way. She had long straight auburn hair that she wore in a knot on top of her head. Black eyelashes framed emerald irises, and she had a sprinkling of freckles across her nose. Eden thought her figure was refreshingly curvy compared to most of the teenage stick insects that pranced around the corridors at her last school. Although her dressing gown didn't do her justice, she had an hour glass silhouette, with ample hips, bust and bottom, and an open face that hid nothing.

As the girls got more acquainted, Eden felt increasingly comfortable in Niamh's company. Eden quickly realised that in complete contrast to her own manner Niamh was devoid of any internal dialogue; every thought that crept into her head came tumbling out of her mouth at a rate of knots. Quite conversely Eden gave very little away, her privacy was her sanctuary. Much like her Father sharing her innermost thoughts and secrets with another person was not an attractive option to Eden, but she couldn't help but find such easy honesty an endearing quality in her new friend. Niamh continued to produce various self-deprecating tales and embarrassing life stories.

"So there I was in the lashing rain waiting for my Mam to pick me up from sailing club. I absolutely love sailing, it's kind of a big deal in our house." Niamh leapt up from the bed. She reached into her suitcase and produced a small blue photo frame which she hurled chaotically over to Eden.

Eden lurched from her position and just about managed to catch it. The picture revealed a slightly sunburnt Niamh as she reclined on the deck of a cabin cruiser. She was looking out to sea wearing a 'My Boat My Rules' T-shirt, and a novelty captain's hat. In the background the sun beat down on the surface of the water. As the warm rays caught the ocean ripples a kaleidoscope of colour was captured on film; it looked like an underwater rainbow.

"That is my baby. Her name is Leviathan. Levi for short. My Dad bought her for me last year, and I have sailed her pretty much every weekend since."

Niamh sat down next to Eden and had another sip of her tea. "Anyway what was I saying? Oh yeah – so I had just finished at the Sailing Club and was absolutely desperate for the loo, and finally I saw my Mam's car pull into the car park. Needless-to-say I dashed into the car and began a long rant about my Mam's lateness, and how I was busting a gut for a wee, before looking over and seeing that I was in fact in the wrong car. My Mam was actually parked two cars behind. To make matters worse the handsome young man next to me was my next door neighbour, so the shame follows me around every day. It was seriously excruciating."

As Niamh regaled tale after tale, Eden giggled and felt her own cheeks going red in sympathy. Two cups of tea and a packet of biscuits later, the girls decided they really must get ready. Eden smiled to herself as Niamh put on some music and danced around their dorm whilst applying her makeup. Worcestershire and her old life felt a long way away.

As the evening drew in, the sun set and the rain began to splatter on the window pain. The murky sky looked almost dystopian, like a scene from a science fiction film. It cozied up to Cantillon like a long lost friend.

Chapter Four

"But isn't it a bit wrong to have a 'Living Dead' Ball in a chapel?" Scotty asked as he cleaned lipstick off his teeth, and approached the bar.

"It's not like you to have any kind of moral barometer," replied Dylan as he looked his friend up and down. "And, anyway, I can't believe you are talking about morality whilst wearing that outfit."

Scotty, in his usual bad taste, had decided to go to the ball dressed as Heath Ledger, when he played The Joker in *The Dark Knight*. The costume consisted of generously applied green eye shadow, red lipstick, sprayed yellow hair, and a female nurse's uniform. Dylan had tried, in vain, to persuade him that dressing as a recently deceased celebrity, a tragic figure even, may be construed as a little ghoulish. However, as they entered Cantillon's chapel, a grand old room, with high ceilings and an impressive stained glass window at its centre, Dylan realised that Scotty's outfit was in good company. Various dead celebrity homages were in attendance including Kurt Cobain complete with gunshot wound, Steve Irwin teamed with blow up crocodile, an undead version of Judy Garland when she played Dorothy Gale in the *Wizard of Oz*, and a crucified Jesus.

Dylan continued to scan the room to see what other morbid creations had been created for the evening. There were the obligatory vampires and zombies, which Dylan found to be a little too obvious, some hideous attempts at Bella and Edward from the *Twilight* Saga, and numerous cult horror tributes including Michael Myers from *Halloween*, Leatherface from *Texas Chainsaw Massacre*, and Freddy Krueger from *A Nightmare on Elm Street*.

Someone had even gone as far as to fashion a real pigs head with long black wig in the style of the horror film *Saw*. Dylan had decided to play it safe and go for a fictional dead character. He was dressed as Kenny from *South Park*, a character that manages to die during every episode. It wasn't an easy feat, but Dylan somehow managed not only to pull it off, but to look good doing it, too. His bright orange hooded jacket and trouser suit should have looked ridiculous, but his broad shoulders, tall build, and dark swarthy looks, just about rescued him from ludicrousy.

Across the room, Scotty spotted a girl in the most outlandish outfit of the evening. She wore a blonde-bobbed wig, white blood-stained jumper, and ripped jeans. Around her neck was a noose tied to a home-made tree stump, ingeniously secured to the back of her costume.

"Drew Barrymore in *Scream*, when she was stabbed and hung from the tree in her garden," Dylan noted immediately. There wasn't much he didn't know about horror films.

"I didn't ask," Scotty replied as he produced a bottle of vodka from under his skirt. He poured a little into their drinks and then raised his glass in a toast to the girl's costume, "but kudos to her". The girl smiled back at him and then turned and laughed with the person behind her. "Now, who is that?"

Dylan followed Scotty's gaze and immediately understood why he was so keen to find out. He couldn't quite see the girl's face, but instantly knew she was beautiful. She looked as if she had been poured into a tiny white lace corset, its sweetheart neckline delicately frayed and torn around the edges, just about protecting her decency, but drawing the eye of every man and woman in the room. A layered skirt floated down to the floor and had been dipped-dyed in midnight blue. Her long hair had a navy sheen that matched the cobalt-blue roses on her headband. She was the Corpse Bride from Tim Burton's film. The boys just gawped.

"See now that's impressive for two reasons. One, she is

sooo hot, and two… well you really don't need a 'two', but you're not getting that getup from Skull Duggery fancy dress shop, now are you?" Scotty looked at Dylan, who had been silent the whole time. He was just watching her.

The high pitched howl of microphone interference jolted the pair back to earth. The DJ's music screeched to a halt. A woman wearing ridiculously shaped glasses and canary yellow hair that was arranged in short frizzy tuffs all over her head began a sound test.

"Testing, testing, 1-2-3." Her eyes darted around the room as she spoke into the microphone, it made a loud shrieking sound that cut through the chapel. The speaker looked slightly deranged.

"Whoops, sorry! Welcome, first years. I am Dora Wilding. I know that I speak for all of the staff here at Cantillon College when I say 'welcome to our happy home'."

Dora then embarked on a very long account of Cantillon's history.

"So, you see, the very building that we are standing in was built by Lord Arthur Westerner in the 1790s and was used as his private residence whilst he courted his mistress Lady Bedford. Lord Westerner was a quirky, frivolous sort, even by today's standards he was rather… adventurous, shall we say."

Dora looked into the crowd. The faces under the elaborate fancy dress make-up looked bored and expressionless. A skinny Marilyn Manson yawned in the distance, as a ginger haired werewolf gave him a nudge.

"Anyway, Lord Westerner's most extravagant venture was to transform the gardens of his estate into a carnival, which the press dubbed the Black Carnival or 'The Carnival Noir' because of its shocking and macabre sideshows, a tradition that can still be seen on the island today. As I am sure you have noticed the Carnival Noir has come to Cantillon once again, and whilst its grave and debauched reputation has thankfully diminished over the years, we wanted to recreate as much of Lord Westerner's Cantillon as possible for you this evening."

"I'll give debauchery a go," Scotty whispered.

"Tonight we come together to celebrate the history of the island and to welcome you to the college, hence our rather ghoulish theme of the Living Dead. You will now be split into your form groups and will take part in the Carnival Noir. Please make the most of this opportunity to get to know your fellow peers. We wish you a very enjoyable, but may I remind you, *safe*, evening."

Dora proceeded on announcing the house groupings. There were three houses in total, which were all named after Catholic saints. Dylan was in the library with Richard Reynolds, whilst Scotty was in the chapel with the rest of John Fisher. Thomas Moore had been asked to congregate in the main hall.

Removing her flower headband nervously, Eden took her seat in the main hall and glanced around the room of strangers. She didn't recognise a single person in Thomas Moore. She wished that Niamh had not been allocated to John Fisher. A petite girl wearing a zombie version of Dorothy from the *Wizard of Oz* tottered over to her. She was clearly struggling to walk in the high-heeled ruby slippers. The girl's face was full of concern.

"Are you alright?" Eden asked as the girl chewed a nail and took the seat next to her.

"I think I might be in the wrong class. I was in the toilets on the phone to my evil stepmother when the groups were called out. Is this John Fisher?"

"I'm afraid this is Thomas Moore. You should have stayed in the chapel."

"Oh, God. I can't possibly walk in late, everyone will look at me. It will be totally mortifying." The girl gulped and the rouge colour on her cheeks deepened. Her brown puppy-dog-eyes became waterlogged.

"Don't panic. I think I noticed a side entrance to the chapel earlier in the evening." Eden looked over at Dora who was on her hands and knees, wrestling with some

23

papers that she had dropped.

"It looks like I have a few minutes before I will be missed. Follow me,' Eden whispered as she jumped up from her seat. She then grabbed the girl's hand, and led her down the corridor into the side entrance of the chapel.

"I am eternally grateful. Thank you. I am Nancy, by the way."

"A pleasure. I am Eden,' she whispered and waved, as Nancy tiptoed into the chapel and slipped into an empty seat next to a handsome boy dressed as The Joker from Batman.

Eden quickly made her way back to the main hall without detection.

"Do you mind if we join your group?" A giggly voice that seemed to come out of nowhere said. "I'm Amira and this is Riley. We just love your Corpse Bride outfit. You look amazing!" Amira's huge dark brown eyes looked almost mahogany in the light.

"Thanks." Eden blushed. She had never been good at dealing with compliments. "I really didn't have a clue what to wear. This corset is killing me." Eden gestured towards the steel ribs that had been stitched into her corset. "These stupid things have been cutting into me all night."

"Darling, with that body you could dress as a lollipop lady and work it," Riley chimed in. Both girls laughed at the thought of it.

Riley's own costume was rather ambiguous. He wore a red tartan kilt with matching sash, dark jacket, and white shirt. He had shaved hair and some subtle eye makeup which gave him that 'just deceased' look. Eden didn't know who he had come as, but thought he looked rather handsome. In contrast, there was no mistaking Amira's outfit. She wore 1920s gangster style shoes that had been customised into stiletto high-heels, her tight cream leather pants hugged her in all the right places, as did her skin tight white blazer. On her head was a white Trilby hat with black trim, she had pushed it over her eyes and her dark brown hair trickled down her back like melting chocolate. It was an impressive take on Michael Jackson's *Smooth Criminal* video.

"Don't worry, no one has guessed my outfit yet." Riley appeared to notice the confused expression on Eden's face. 'I'm Alexander McQueen. You know, the fashion designer who died a while back?"

Fashion was not Eden's forte but she recognised the name of the late fashion designer and seemed to remember that he was of Scottish heritage.

"Well we may not have guessed who you are dressed as, but you pull off the kilt and sash very well." Eden smiled at him, her words seemed to lift his spirits. "So I guess we should head over to the Carnival Noir then," Eden's voice was clearly apprehensive.

"It all looks a bit scary to me," Amira said meekly.

"Indeed we should…," agreed Riley, as he put his arm around Amira's shoulder and whispered, "let the games begin…," in the voice of Jigsaw from the horror film *Saw*.

"Riley! Stop scaring me." Amira kicked him in the shin and linked arms with Eden. Riley hobbled along behind them.

The Carnival Noir was a veritable delight. Eden looked deep into the crowd and was met with the most vivacious colours and textures. A young trapeze artist shimmered in a metallic bikini, and giggled as she grabbed the hand of her silver-haired, strong shouldered team mate as they danced off into the big-top tent. Sword swallowers stood on stilts with their matching connoisseur moustaches, their blades glimmered in the moonlight. In perfect synchronicity they raised the swords above their head and plunged them through their open mouths, deep into their stomachs. Eden winced.

As the sword swallowers proudly took a bow, Eden noticed a circus clown in the distance. Eden shuddered. She had always found clowns creepy and this one seemed to be made from the stuff of nightmares. Its black eyes bore into her, it stretched its bright red lips into a grimace, revealing spiky fanged teeth. It stared at her for a long moment. The wind-up music box, which was gleefully chanting away, fell silent and, for a split second, Eden had the overwhelming sensation to run. But a second later the sword swallowers resumed their position, and the clown was gone.

A hand appeared on Eden's shoulder. She jumped and spun around to see Riley's huge grin.

"You have got to see this, it's so wrong it's amazing!"

Eden breathed out a sigh of relief as Riley and Amira grabbed her hand and dragged her into a striped tent with the word 'Freaks' written above the door.

Inside, the room was packed with people. The jubilant crowd were laughing and jeering at a pot-bellied man dressed as a ringmaster.

"Ladies and Gentleman, tonight we are going to experience the weird, the wonderful and the darn right odd. These are the creatures from the darkest corners of the world and they have gathered here this evening for your pleasure. Everything you see before you is one-hundred percent authentic. There have been no special effects or temporary make-up used. These people live their lives as you see them here tonight. Enchanted audience, I give you, THE FREAKS!"

The audience erupted in gleeful applause.

"If I see one little person I'm out of here." Eden said pointedly, finding the whole concept rather exploitative and distasteful.

Riley was too busy whistling at the stage to even acknowledge Eden's concern.

The red velvet curtains opened, and at the centre of the stage stood a huge glass container that resembled a display case. It was filled with smoke. Strobe lights flickered and music pumped out of two huge speakers.

"For one night only, plucked straight out of Greek mythology, please welcome The Centaur." The Ringmaster announced in a booming voice.

The smoke cleared and standing in the centre of the display was a sight that Eden never dreamed possible. The long haired man was exceptionally well built; he was bare-chested and glistening under the lights. But it was not his sculpted physique that drew the attention of the crowd. The Centaur's legs were entirely covered in thousands of tiny brown horse hairs that had been individually implanted beneath the skin, giving the overall impression of a glossy coat. His lower calves and ankles had been broken, modified, and stretched to take on the appearance of a horse's rear. He turned around and lifted his taut, bent legs to reveal the horse shoes that had been moulded to the bottom of his feet. Amira wolf-whistled at the stage, and the crowd made noises of delight. Eden just stared on in shock, until the smoke enveloped him once more.

The house lights went out.

Eden moved closer to Riley, as the crowd fell silent. A single tiny light began to dance amidst the fog. Gradually a woman's silhouette came into view. She was ultra feminine - small framed but curvaceous, with long hair that trailed the bottom of her back. The woman appeared to be wearing the most intricately designed floral leotard, but as the light intensified, Eden noticed that she was naked, and her entire body had been tattooed in flowers. Amidst her long-flowing violet hair were two beautiful feathered angel wings which were surgically implanted into her shoulder blades. As she turned, she raised a hand to her ear to demonstrate their elvish shape.

"Ladies and Gentleman, I give you, Angelica."

Eden thought she was beautiful.

The ringmaster cleared his throat once more. "And now, from the truly sublime to the somewhat ridiculous. Please show your appreciation for the British treasure, I give you, Pigeon Man."

Eden rolled her eyes as a ridiculous looking man covered in grey pigeon feathers and a bright orange beak, hopped onto the stage.

"On that note, I'm most definitely off," Eden shouted to Riley and Amira over the applause. "I'll meet you both back at the sword swallowers."

Riley's eyes didn't leave the stage. He shooed her away,

captivated by the most recent abomination.

Eden slid out of the crowded tent as quickly as she could. She had never enjoyed packed spaces and gasped the fresh air as she spilled onto the cobbled pavement and into the night. Disorientated, she glanced around and realised that she must have taken the wrong exit. Eden began to wander around in search of a clear route back to the Carnival Noir, but along the way she stumbled upon the stone steps that led down to Cantillon Beach.

The sea called to her. The quiet, calmness of the ocean was so appealing amidst the loud, garish chaos of the carnival. Eden needed five minutes' solitude. It had been years since she felt the sand between her toes, and smelled the salty sea air. She hadn't realised how much she had missed it. Her legs began to walk towards the stone steps, almost of their own accord. Eden removed her heels and began to negotiate the jagged shoreline. The rocks snagged her dress and grazed her skin, but it was more than worth it to be back on the beach again.

Eden looked out across the water that glistened below the moon. She had always loved her own company and couldn't remember a time when she felt more content. Having always worried so much about what others thought of her, Eden considered that happiness was achieved most easily in solitude. These moments alone with nature, allowed a sense of inner calm.

Eden walked down the old wooden pier, hitched up her skirt and sat carefully on the edge. The cold snap stung her toes as she dipped them into the black water. It was completely still. Tiny fish gathered around and tickled her ankles; their tiny kisses soothed the cuts she endured on the climb down. Eden closed her eyes and just sat there for a long moment and drifted off into daydreams.

Drip, drip.

Eden was abruptly awoken from thought, she opened her eyes slowly.

Drip, drip.

What on earth was that noise? Eden thought as she

looked around, but saw nothing.

The noise became louder. Eden was convinced something or someone had emerged from under the water and was coming towards her, but there was nothing there.

Drip, drip.

There it was again. Eden sat forward, she felt a chill. She didn't know whether to be excited or afraid. *Was this a seal or a dolphin in the distance, diving in and out the water, making a show just for her?* Eden couldn't shake the overwhelming feeling that something was terribly wrong. She had seen one too many *Jaws* movies. But this was the British Coast, she scolded herself, it was hardly California.

Drip, drip.

The breath caught in Eden's throat. She froze.

A huge black shadow glided under the surface just inches away from her feet.

Despite the instinct to pull her legs out of the water as fast as she could, Eden knew she must evade the creature's detection.

She began to slowly lift her feet from the water.

But it was too late.

It grabbed hold of her ankle and pulled her hard into the blackness.

Before Eden could react she was submerged in the ocean, she began to choke.

The salt water stabbed at her eyes, but she forced them open as she furiously tried to identify her assailant.

Her ankle began to pulse with pain. *Had something bitten her?*

Eden kicked as hard as she could, but it had her in a vice like grip, pulling deeper and deeper into the abyss. Her heart felt like it was going to explode. Water ran down the back of her throat. Panic set in. The ivory wedding dress danced around in the black water, billowing out like an aquatic ghost; she yanked it away from her face.

Think, Eden. Think. You can get out of this, you are not an idiot in some horror movie, you are better than that. What do you need to do? And then an idea came.

She needed something sharp and fast. Eden remembered her Corpse Bride costume, and the metallic ribs. She pulled at the corset with all her might, and finally fashioned herself a weapon.

Now for the really difficult bit. In a split second Eden managed to bend over so her arms were hugging her knees. She could see nothing but blackness. She got as close to her ankles as possible, drew back her weapon and plunged it hard into her attacker. Blood seeped into the water, and finally it relinquished its grasp.

Eden frantically clawed her way back to the surface; she could feel the water movements underneath her as the creature followed rapidly in her wake. Finally she reached the pier again and gasped the air. She grabbed the wooden boardwalk and tried to hurl her body out of the water, but something was weighing her down. At first she thought it was just the drag of the water, but then to Eden's complete confusion, she realised she was entirely covered in the most rancid smelling sticky slime. It felt like being covered in a slippery cocoon, or hundreds of spider's webs. *What on earth was it?* It was all over her face, in her mouth, she could taste it, it clung to her wet body like a second skin. *Was it skin?* She frantically peeled it off, but there was so much of it.

Bubbles sprang up from the murky depths, the black mass was gaining on her. She scrambled to free herself from her milky prison. The heavens opened and rain poured from the swelling black sky, it washed the remnants of the putrid substance away. Eden ran deeper and deeper into the night. She didn't know where her attacker was but she wasn't going to stop and find out. She stumbled upon a dilapidated old cabin with boarded-up windows that must have been an old Carnival attraction. Outside, the name, 'The Banshee's Burrow' hung above the door. Eden felt terrified at the prospect of having to enter.

A branch snapped behind her.

Instinct to survive drove her forward into the blackness. She must find a place to hide. She stretched her arms out and entered the Banshee's Burrow. Once inside, she shut the door and paused for a few moments, waiting for her eyes to catch up with the rest of her body and adjust to the dark. The black fog was incessant, it felt as though she was wearing a blindfold. She fumbled around for a few moments, desperately searching for somewhere to hide.

Suddenly a beam of light penetrated the darkness. The cabin door creaked as it opened and closed.

The creature was in there with her.

Eden groped around and felt a cold metallic banister leading down into a basement. She had nowhere else to go, choking back tears of terror she clung to the handrail and eased her way down the first step. Devoid of sight, she relied on her other senses to guide her. The smell of mould filled her nostrils. Everywhere felt damp and clammy.

She could hear a drip, drip, drip from behind her.

And then... A blood-curdling scream echoed throughout the cabin. It sounded like a woman wailing.

It was too much to bear. Eden spun around and ran frantically away from the terrifying sound, tears pouring down her cheeks. In the dark she crashed into something cold and hard. A dim light switched on and Eden realised she was pressed up against a glass cabinet. Every hair on the back of her neck prickled, as she found herself face to face with a wrinkled old woman wearing a black lace veil. The woman stared at Eden, then raised her head, opened her mouth and let out the most horrifying scream.

Eden fell to the ground. As she put her hands out to break her fall, she dislodged a plug socket from the wall. In an instant the cabinet fell into darkness and the screaming was silenced.

Of course! The veiled woman was a manikin. It must have been the Banshee from the Banshee's Burrow, just another fake attraction from the Carnival Noir.

Eden remembered learning about the Banshee in Irish History, and how they were mythical creatures that began to wail when someone was going to die. To hear the scream of the Banshee meant that you were almost certainly going to meet your end.

Eden gulped. Someone had deliberately switched on the attraction. Whatever was in there with her was trying to terrify her, and they were doing a good job of it so far.

She had to get out of there.

Eden pulled herself to her feet and groped around for the bannister that would lead her out of this god-awful place. A table, a large coat stand, and then her fingertips traced something soft and shiny. Eden left her hands there a moment, attempting to decipher what it was.

And then she knew.

She flinched and jumped back, as her whole body went cold.

The object at her fingertips was warm. She was touching a human face, with long, thick, dripping wet hair. And this time it was no manikin.

Deep, raspy breath filled Eden's ears. A bony hand grabbed her own, it clung to her in a vice-like grip. Eden screamed and flung her whole body back. She hit something and for a split second light flooded into the room. In one petrifying moment, she saw it. A mass of black, long hair hung over a ghostly white face. Blue veins pulsed under the translucent skin. Eden could just about make out two of the blackest eyes she had ever seen. They didn't seem human. They were wild somehow, almost reptilian.

Eden was in blackness once again.

She scrambled frantically back to the light source to try and escape its grasp. The image of those black eyes burnt into her retinas. She pressed her fingers against a wooden object, that felt like a small boarded up window. She shoved it as hard as she could and began to scramble through. The angle was virtually impossible. She put her feet through first, and then her hands, but her shoulders got stuck and her upper body was trapped motionless in the room.

The breathing came closer and closer. She could smell its rancid breath. Her hands were trapped, she couldn't protect herself, she just lay there thrashing violently around in the dark. It knew she was captive.

It slowly approached her and made a strange, gravelly almost chuckling sound, as it laid a claw-like hand on her hair and began to stroke it. Bony fingers made their way up to her face, they touched her cheeks, but Eden could do nothing but scream and thrash around. She wasn't going to go down without a fight. She gave one last push and yelped in pain as the broken glass splintered into her stomach. Blood oozed from the wound. The red velvety liquid covered her skin and acted as a lubricant, allowing her to slip her torso through the window to freedom.

As she escaped the creature's grasp, she knocked it off balance. It fell backwards and made an abhorrent, guttural sound. Eden hurled her body faster than her feet could carry her, half running and half falling, she collapsed to the ground.

She heard footsteps, but they were too close for her to run. She kept her head down, her eyes fixed to the ground, she was too terrified to lift them and to see her attacker. Two strong hands were upon her now, lifting her to her feet. She had nothing left, she relinquished all control and surrendered.

Chapter Five

Dylan didn't know what had hit him. Under the mass of brown hair, he looked down to see familiar wide green eyes, meeting his own. An uncanny feeling swept through him. These eyes were known to him; emeralds that he used to think about all the time. He had nearly convinced himself that they didn't exist, that he made them up, but there they were, after all this time. They were changed somehow, older, and somehow sadder but, nevertheless, they were hers. He didn't know how or why, but *she* was with him once again.

Eden looked at Dylan for a long moment and soon realised that she had lingered in his embrace for quite some time, without a word of explanation. She readjusted herself and stepped away. The world which had been moving in slow motion skipped back to real time. Rain beat down on them, she was out of breath, she looked around, but there was no sign of her assailant.

"Oh my god, I'm sorry. I just had such a fright, there was someone in there with me, they grabbed me,' she continued to scan the area. "Where are they? Did they follow me? They tried to…" Eden broke off, she was frantic.

"Eden,' the sound of his voice stopped her in her tracks. His strong hands gripped her shoulders as he guided her under a tree to find shelter. He took off his jacket and placed it on the base of the tree trunk. They sat down together. "I can't believe you're here. What on earth happened…" Dylan had so many questions.

She looked into his eyes.

"Sorry Dylan. I'm just so..." Her voice cracked as she flopped down to sit on the floor. The lunacy of the whole situation finally got to her and she buried her face in her hands. Tears came easily. This was not how it was supposed to be. When she pictured this moment—*the* moment - when they were reunited, she imagined herself as calm, together, mature, not a tearful mess. "I can't believe I am crying. I never cry'. Eden was overwhelmed by how emotional she felt. It was as if Dylan had unlocked a secret vault and everything came flooding out. The kindness in his gentle, handsome face that had become a man since she saw him last, seemed to rob her of all strength and pretence. Without saying a word, he wrapped an arm around her and they just sat there. Raindrops danced on the leaves, and darkness fell around them.

"You are bleeding." Dylan put his hand on her stomach and looked closely at the wound. He winced, "it looks deep, we need to get you cleaned up and someone needs to take a look at that. What actually happened? Tell me from the beginning." Dylan began to stand up.

"Can we just stay here for a moment? I need everything to stop, just for a little while."

Dylan settled back down on his jacket.

"I just don't know what happened. One minute I was sitting on the pier and the next, something pulled me into the water. I managed to get away, but then there was this stuff. This weird, slimy grossness that was all over me as I tried to get out of the sea. I got most of it off me, and then tried to hide in that old crappy house, which would quite frankly terrify the bejesus out of Count Dracula," Eden's speech was broken and her tone verged on hysterical, "and then it followed me in there. It had the coldest, darkest eyes that I have ever seen. I don't even know if it was human."

"Slow down, slow down. If it wasn't human, then what else could it have been?"

"I don't know, maybe I'm just crazy and imagined the whole thing. I have been feeling weird for a few days." The strange sighting from her dormitory window came into her mind.

Dylan took Eden's hands reassuringly. "The cut on your stomach would suggest otherwise. We need to report this to the police,"

"And say what exactly? That I got slimed, and that something that I can't even be sure was human, tried to drown me for no apparent reason. They'll have me committed. I can't call the police and cause a huge fuss on my first night here. My parents would… I just can't."

"You can and you must, Eden. Whatever this is could try and hurt you again."

"Please don't push me on this. My parents aren't exactly delighted with my decision to come back. I won't be calling anyone."

Dylan was not convinced, but Eden's eyes willed him to move on.

The conversation fell silent.

Eden knew what was coming next. He would have to ask her. If she were in his position she would have done so already. And then the questioning came.

"Eden…," Dylan raised his eyes from the sodden ground to look deep into hers, "what happened to you? I mean that night, all those years ago? Where did you go?" Dylan was not sure if he really wanted to know.

Eden averted his gaze.

After all this time, Dylan had convinced himself of so many scenarios – her father got a new job, a grandparent became ill – all of which left Eden to live a relatively happy existence. He was so afraid that the truth would be comparatively more sinister.

"We moved to Worcestershire, I didn't know anything about it until that night, I cried the whole journey." Eden's answer offered very little in unravelling the mystery.

"I knocked on your door every day for a month." They both smiled warmly. "Why did your parents need to leave in such a hurry, without a word to anyone, it just didn't make any sense? Your house, your belongings, were all still there, just as you left them?"

Eden knew he would ask, but that didn't make it easier to find answers. She didn't want to lie to him, but the truth was not an option.

Silence fell once again.

"Okay, I get it. You don't have to go into it, but please know that if you ever want to, no matter how awful you think it is, I am here. Well, not literally here." He gestured to the spot they were sitting in. "I would get chilly and hungry, but you know what I mean, metaphorically speaking."

Eden laughed and remembered how he could always make her smile.

A shrill sound of a bell ringing echoed through the island, beckoning the cohort back to the chapel. They both looked at each other and sighed. Neither wanted to go back. Dylan rose to his feet and outstretched his hand to Eden. She took it.

And at that moment, the rain stopped beating down.

***

Nancy Grange didn't want to leave the Living Dead party early. So what if she had gym practice in the morning? She was so tired of the training, the competitions, she was even tired of the trophies, and she despised her stepmother for pushing her so hard. Didn't Mary realise how freakish Nancy would look, taking public transport in the pouring rain in this ridiculous costume? Next year she would definitely board at Cantillon dormitories. Nancy's thoughts were interrupted as she caught one of her ruby slippers on the stone staircase and slipped halfway down the steps. Her gingham pinafore dress stuck to her knees and her French plaits dripped water down her face into her eyes. Her dark zombie eye makeup stung her eyelashes.

"Just fabulous." She spat the words as she stomped along. Why didn't Dorothy Gale carry an umbrella? Nancy was sure there were all sorts of weather problems in Kansas, not to mention the merry old Land of Oz. She made her way to the harbour, taking the shortcut through the cemetery.

But then she heard a strange sound.

It sounded like something had crawled or slithered over the wet leaves.

Nancy glanced around, but nothing was out of place. In this weather there were lots of odd noises, she may have even imagined it.

The interruption did begin to make her feel a little uneasy. Her irritated mood had distracted her from focusing on the here and now, and she suddenly felt vulnerable and alone.

Little Dorothy Gale, lit up like a beacon amongst this vast and dreary landscape. She looked up at the starless sky, it was so black on the island, not like Skull with all its street lights.

Nancy's ruby slippers quickened as they drew nearer the harbour, she could see the lights shining through the rain in the distance, she relaxed her shoulders a little, she hadn't realised how tense she had become.

"It's just a bit of rain," she sighed.

But then she heard it again.

It was unmistakable this time, and so very much nearer. Her stomach jerked. Her breath caught in her throat.

She was not going to wait around to hear it again. Her ruby slippers began to pick up pace, the harbour was so close, she could almost touch it. She began to feel relief. Everything was about to be okay.

She was nearly there.

The slippers moved faster still, she held her breath and began to have the courage to glance around.

And that is when she froze.

The sound of breathing was just behind her.

She could feel it on her neck.

Her breath stopped dead in her throat, and then she saw it.

The last thing she would ever see.

Her mouth curled into a silent scream, her little gingham pinafore crumpled, as her body hit the ground with a thud.

Chapter Six

The room was cold. He could see his own breath. He rubbed his hands together for warmth and snuggled into his coat as he approached the bed. Her tiny frame lay there, she was still a child. Her skin was so pale it was almost blue. Her cheeks were slashed and bore sores where freckles used to be, they oozed with blood and puss. Her white nightgown was drenched in pea green vomit. Her dead eyes rolled back in her head, as she shed her shackles. And then she rose into the air and levitated.

Dr Justin Entwistle paused the horror film. At twenty-nine he was moderately attractive, but after last night's bottle of wine he had seen better days. He hoped the students couldn't smell alcohol on his breath, Cantillon had a reputation to uphold, and his penchant for socialising with some of the female students had already drawn too much attention from Principal Duggan; Justin couldn't add alcoholism to the list.

"William Friedkin's *The Exorcist* is one of the scariest movies of all time. The film is an intriguing insight into America in 1973, and cultural issues of divorce, working mothers, Catholicism and the role of faith versus science in the modern world. But what is truly fascinating, in terms of horror, is the transformation sequences – the grotesque, abject possession of Regan, this is Body Horror at its best."

Justin scanned the room, they appeared to be listening, a novelty in his profession. He refrained from getting too elated, it was the first week of term after all. By week five, two-thirds of them would invariably start writing notes to each other, or fall asleep on their desks, whilst the other third may not even turn up at all. The modern education system he thought, best make the most of it now.

"So as film students, what other examples of Body Horror – the familiar made strange – have you seen that top Friedkin's head spinning, crucifix wielding, twelve-year-old?" Justin invited an attractive blonde to contribute.

"Friedkin has nothing on Landis, and *American Werewolf in London*. When David turns into a werewolf it is seriously messed up, it looks agonising. The sequence is so long and drawn out, that you almost experience the sensation of bones stretching, bending, and breaking with him."

Dylan swivelled in his seat to view the speaker in more detail. She was stunning, in an unconventional sense, which gave her an exotic mystique. She had sandy hair and dark tanned skin and wore a black sweetheart corset with a long skirt. Her eyes melted into dark makeup, and her silver bracelets jangled as she spoke. Dylan couldn't stop himself from joining the debate.

"That *Blue Moon* sequence in *American Werewolf in London* is a defining moment in horror for sure. In fact you could say it was pivotal to popular culture in general, what with Michael Jackson's *Thriller* video also directed by Landis, and the endless zombie parodies," Dylan forgot himself for a moment and continued. "But for me, David Cronenberg is the true master of the genre, *Videodrome*, *Shivers*, *Rabid*. The part when he pulls his own fingernails off in *The Fly* is brilliant, my little sister didn't sleep for weeks after I showed her that!" Dylan hoped he didn't look too much of a geek, but he was not used to talking about horror film to people who didn't yawn, or change the subject at the first opportunity. He had a strict Catholic education, and debating body horror scenes from *The Exorcist* just didn't feature on the curriculum.

Scotty raised his hand.

Dylan knew nothing good would come from allowing Scotty to contribute to the, so far, highbrow intellectual exchange.

Justin scanned the room for the next comment. "Yes, erm," he checked the register, "Liam Scott,"

"Two words for you, Justin my man – the *Human Centipede.*"

"That's three," Dylan quipped and the class erupted in laughter.

"On that note, I would say that's lunch." Justin was suddenly very aware that the discussion was pushing a few too many boundaries.

Justin began collecting up his notes as the class slowly trundled out the lecture hall. He could hear a student explaining the plot of the *Human Centipede* to his friends as they made noises of revulsion. Justin's thoughts were interrupted as a dark haired beauty appeared at his desk; she wore a tight T-shirt with a large green apple printed on the front. He smiled to himself; giving a teacher an apple took on a whole new meaning.

"Thank you for that Justin, the discussion was really interesting." Amira leaned over his desk to reveal her full cleavage.

"That's err …" Justin's voice cracked, he cleared his throat, "I'm glad you thought so. And who might you be?"

"I'm Amira Acharya".

Riley watched from the doorway, and rolled his eyes. "Here we go again," he muttered under his breath.

Dylan and Scotty wandered out to the gardens. The sun beat down on them, there was no sign of yesterday's rain, a typical British summer.

"Sorry, Dylan, is it?" Dylan turned to see the sandy haired girl from earlier. "I'm Oregan. I just wanted to say I love Cronenberg too, none of my friends have even heard of him."

Dylan couldn't quite believe that someone that looked like Oregan would be talking to him. Up close she was even more beautiful. Dylan blushed and averted her gaze, his eyes wandered to the tattoo she had on the inside of her wrist, it was a Great White Shark swimming through pink roses. He tried to disguise the fact he was staring at it. This girl was so unique.

"In fact," Oregan continued, twisting her silver bracelets as she spoke, "Cronenberg"s *Videodrome* is playing on the mainland on Saturday if you fancy catching it? I was going to go anyway."

Dylan was a little stunned by her directness, was this a date? He weighed up the situation; on the one-hand the last thing he wanted to do was muddy the waters with Eden, but on the other, a new college friend would be nice, and particularly one this intriguing. Either way, Dylan didn't have any more time to deliberate this, his pregnant pause was becoming awkward.

"Of course. Sounds like a plan." As the words came out of his mouth he immediately wished he could push them back in. He took Oregan's number and she disappeared as quickly as she arrived.

Scotty smacked Dylan in the arm.

"Ouch, what did you do that for?"

"Sorry mate," Scotty said "I had to check I was still here. Cantillon seems to be a strange upside down world where *you* are hot, and I am ... well not." Even entertaining the thought seemed a travesty to Scotty. "I thought college was supposed to be a girl fest, so far I am seeing slim pickings my friend. Last night you are having deep and meaningfuls with Eden in the rain, she is a 'worldy' by the way."

Dylan understood another of Scotty's made-up words to mean 'out of this world.'

"And now you have got a date with Oregan, who is possibly a little psycho, but still, with her looks she can afford to be. Maybe it's the whole strong silent thing that you have going on, I'm gonna try that."

Scotty and Dylan were so involved in their conversation that they didn't notice they had stumbled into two of their classmates eating lunch. A gargantuan stone water feature of two battling sea gods dwarfed Riley and Amira as they tucked into their sandwiches. Eden and Niamh approached in the distance.

"Hi." Dylan smiled warmly at Eden, and for a split second it felt as though it was just the two of them. "Ouch." Dylan was dragged immediately back down to earth by Scotty, who was pinching his arm. "Sorry, Eden this is my friend Scotty."

"Hi, Scotty. Lovely to meet you," Eden said warmly.

Scotty muttered a vague "hi" in response, but barely acknowledged Eden's existence. Eden looked a little hurt and perplexed.

Dylan read Scotty like a book and whispered under his breath, "do the strong silent thing another time, you are coming across weird."

Scotty immediately resumed his usual wide grin, and loud but loveable manner. "Sorry Eden, darling, lovely to meet you." Scotty had the ability to brighten up any situation, his smile was infectious. He outstretched his hand, but then changed his mind and pulled Eden in for a bear hug. "Oh what the hell. Dylan's friends are my friends, right?"

Eden smiled as she unpeeled herself from Scotty's rather random embrace. "This is my room-mate, Niamh. I think you guys had Film Studies with Amira and Riley?" The boys nodded in confirmation.

"So how are you doing after last night?" Dylan asked.

"Yes, Eden. What exactly happened last night?" Riley said putting down his sandwich. "We waited for ages, but then bumped into some friends of Amira's and thought we had missed you."

Eden took a deep breath and recounted last night's sequence of events to the group.

"Well that's certainly the freakiest thing I have heard in a long time," Scotty said with his usual sledgehammer tact, not sparing a thought for Eden's feelings.

Dylan shot him a look.

"Crap. Sorry, Eden. But you have to admit its right up there with spotting UFOs and seeing Jesus's face in a potato," Scotty said, not making it any better.

Amira choked back a laugh.

"It does sound a little far-fetched in the cold light of day, but that's how it happened." Eden shrugged.

"You have to report it, Eden. God knows what could have happened if Dylan hadn't arrived when he did." Niamh beamed a smile in Dylan's direction, a genuine gesture for protecting their mutual friend.

"I can't. I don't want the police to call my parents."

"What if we just speak to our tutors then and leave out the police for now? We need someone to watch your back," Dylan offered, relieving Eden of the pressure to contact the authorities.

Eden bit her bottom lip as her eyes stared at the grass below her feet. Finally she nodded in agreement.

"That's settled then," Riley intercepted before Eden could answer. "We shall take action, and it's up to me to organise you lot."

Whilst donkey work was not his forte, Riley enjoyed orchestrating schemes and generally bossing people around. He was a hard task master, but his heart was in the right place. "Right then," Riley checked his watch. "It's 1300 hours. We all have classes until 1700 hours, correct?"

"You mean five o'clock," Amira agreed. "And yes, we have Film Production with Dylan and Scotty, Eden and Niamh have Geology." Amira acted as Miss Moneypenny to Riley's James Bond.

"So after that we should split up into two groups so we can cover all bases. Eden, you should go to see Dora Wilding and report the incident. Take Dylan with you – he's an official witness. Amira, Niamh and I will go to the security cabin and see if we can access the footage from last night. We might be able to spot your attacker leaving the carnival for the beach."

Scotty gave a loud cough.

"God. Sorry. Scotty is it? Yes I forgot about you." Riley grimaced in embarrassment. "Please do come with us. We could use as many eyes as possible."

Scotty shot Dylan a look and then silently looked down

at his own body as if checking he was still visible.

Dylan chuckled to himself.

"Thanks so much for your help Riley but, realistically, do you really think Cantillon security are going to let a bunch of students into the porter cabin to view the security tape?" Eden asked.

"Eden, darling, firstly 'tape?' This isn't the seventies. Haven't you heard of a little something called the digital revolution? And secondly, those friends of Amira's that we bumped into last night were Cantillon Security. Whilst you were getting felt up by Voldermort, Amira was doing the same with one of the security guys. I spent a good hour or so hanging outside the security cabin."

"Riley!" Amira hit him in the chest, "it really wasn't like that. That makes me sound like a complete..." she trailed off, her face burning.

"We don't think anything of the sort Amira," Niamh said as she shot Riley a look. Niamh was naturally compassionate by nature, and enjoyed being able to scorn Riley.

"Okay. So Eden and I will meet the rest of you guys in the security cabin after we see Dora." Dylan maintained composure, but inwardly was delighted that an opportunity to spend time with Eden had arisen.

"Sorted," Riley concluded, and the group disbanded.

Scotty decided it might be a good idea to walk Amira to class.

The early evening Cantillon ferry set sail for Skull. Two little boys were giggling as they bounced a ball back and forth on the deck. Their mothers chatted and leaned over the railings as they looked out to sea. Cantillon became a dark blob on the horizon. The boys' giggles became louder, and without warning a gust of wind blew across the sea. They lost control of their ball, watching in fear as it soared through the sky and struck an elderly man in the centre of his forehead. His wife jumped up and came to his aid, berating the boys from a distance. This was the last straw.

45

After a telling off, the boys were ordered to sit quietly below deck, much to the elderly couple's delight. The boys stomped down the stairs.

As soon as their mothers were out of sight, they became embroiled in their next adventure. They lay face down on the glass bottom ferry and began taunting the fish. The smallest of the two boys was quite taken with a brown and white sea-snake.

"Look, Callum. That snake is called Sweetie."

"That's an eel, not a snake," said the older boy.

"No it isn't. It's a snake. Sweetie the snake."

The boys continued to argue as they watched the snake swim closer to the glass. They began to mimic its breathing as it grew nearer and nearer. Suddenly it turned and swam behind some rocks. The little boys watched with intrigue, hoping it would come out the other side. But Sweetie had disappeared.

They waited patiently… right up until the screaming began.

The boys looked around blankly but couldn't identify what all the noise was about. Their mothers frantically hurled them up into their arms, carrying them swiftly to the other side of the ferry.

"What is it, Mummy? Are we sinking?" The boy stared intently into his mother's eyes.

The elderly man stepped carefully down the stairs to see what the commotion was about. There, looking straight at him from the sea bed, nestled in some seaweed, was Dorothy from the *Wizard of Oz*. Her silvery eyes were wide open, her plaits danced to the rhythm of the ocean. Her face was mottled, and her skin was so transparent it revealed a network of thick blue veins, which were rendered useless now. The elderly man looked down at her feet, immediately regretting his decision. But it was too late. In a cruel sense of irony, one of her ruby slippers was missing, along with her foot, ankle, and most of her leg.

A bloody stump was all that remained.

There, feasting on the flesh, was Sweetie. He nibbled

contently as his tummy grew fat. Amongst the chaos no-one noticed the sandy haired stranger in the black sweetheart corset that was sitting in the corner. Her back was rigid, her eyelids were closed, but flickered as if she was catatonic. Her lips moved quickly but silently. She put her arms out in front of her body like tentacles; they were bent at strange, unnatural angles. Her bracelets jangled rhythmically and danced around her shark tattoo as the ferry rode the waves.

Chapter Seven

Eden and Dylan took the scenic route through the garden to Dora's office. The silence was beginning to get uncomfortable. Eden didn't know where to start. They had so many years to catch up on, but part of her was terrified to speak. She had thought about him every day since she had left. At that moment, everything was unsaid she could allow herself to get swept away with the drama and the dreaminess of it all. It was all sheer anticipation. She feared that when they spoke the reality might not live up to the fiction and that they might just plummet into ordinariness. She wanted so desperately to preserve these moments, to savour them, as any moment beyond this may not be so close to perfect. The silences they shared seemed to almost be worth more than words, as in those silences he seemed to quietly understand her, she was terrified that all this may get lost in translation.

The logical, pragmatic side to Eden knew that they couldn't exist on memories alone. In order to be important to each other's present, and hopefully future, they had to build a new relationship. As adults they were strangers. They both had different experiences that altered them from those two innocent children so many years ago. Eden knew that she had changed, but it was not for the better. She was haunted by her previous self, and the fun loving, strong-minded girl she used to be. Now she felt damaged. Since that night, years ago, darkness had crept into her, and twisted around her very bones. It had been there so long it strangled her; she no longer knew how to pluck it out, to extract it.

Deep down in her most lucid moments she knew that

the darkness would stop her from being with him in the end.

Dylan looked out to sea and watched the ferry crossing. He decided it was time to break the silence.

"That's odd. That ferry seems to have docked in the middle of the ocean."

Eden woke from her thoughts and followed Dylan's gaze. "That's strange. Maybe they are waiting for a signal or something?"

Dylan nodded his head in agreement.

"So…" Dylan's tone acknowledged the awkwardness.

"How do you even begin to cover five years in as many minutes?" Eden asked.

Dylan cleared his throat grandly as if he was about to make an important speech. "Right, well, I will give it a go. So… parents argued, Dad had an affair with an old flame, parents divorce. Skulldonian FC won the Sunday league, first girlfriend arrives on the scene, first girlfriend quickly exits the scene. Dog dies, start college, crazy girl runs into me, turns my world upside down. And I decide to do this ridiculous speech."

Eden's laughter caught in her throat as he delivered the last few lines. "Okay, well that about covers it." Eden was impressed. "Right, so where shall I start? Moved to Worcestershire, hated Worcestershire. Started new school, hated new school. Parents argue, parents stay together in separate rooms. Got into storm chasing of all things, gave up on boys altogether, applied for college, parents all but disown me, start college, get attacked by a crazy person, would have escaped quicker but silly boys gets in my way."

Dylan feigned being heartbroken.

"And finally, walks through a garden with a boy, and feels as happy as a seven-year-old collecting insects."

They smiled deeply and for a few moments just existed together, content.

"So storm chasing? That's different. I remember that you were always a little bit suicidal when it came to watching thunderstorms on your roof, but storm chasing? That's a different level."

"I know, I know it"s geeky, but there you go. I better fess up now rather than risk you finding out later. When we moved to Worcestershire I had no friends and there was nothing else to do. There was this colossal tornado there years ago, and once I started to learn a little about it, I kinda got sucked in. It's seriously addictive. I guess it's like any extreme sport, people are not often put in a position where nature is threatening them, and I think there is something about that feeling you get, when you watch extreme weather, that makes you feel so small and fragile, it's exciting. It's like swimming with sharks. I am hoping to go to America and do a Meteorology degree." Eden caught herself. She was beginning to sound obsessed. "Anyway, what about you with your horror films? When did you get so into the morbid stuff? A little birdie tells me that you dominated the discussion in class this morning."

"Look at us all grown up. It seems we have both gotten weirder with age."

"Maybe a little geekier. But we were hardly normal children!"

"True," agreed Dylan, his eyes smiling.

"I'm sorry about your parents Dylan. I wouldn't have seen that coming."

"Neither did Mum"

"Were you, I mean, *are* you okay?"

"Yeah. It wasn't great at the time, but Scotty was a real help, accidentally I'm sure. It didn't help that Dad felt the need to justify it to me and Beth. He wanted us to meet his new girlfriend, have dinners together. But how could I, when every night I saw what it was doing to Mum? I just wanted to be a kid again. It's better now though, they can be civil and he has married his other woman now. And Mum, well she has moved Nan in." Dylan realised that this was the first time he had talked about his parents' divorce. He had dreaded the subject coming up for so long. Yet now he felt like he could have talked for hours. He wanted to tell her everything.

"Your Nan is living with you! Lucky old Judy." Eden

remembered Dylan's grandmother was on the eccentric side when they were children, she wondered how the years had affected her.

"Sorry to hear your parents aren't great either. Why are they so upset that you wanted to come back?" Dylan asked.

"God knows," Eden lied. "I think they are just a bit uncomfortable about the thought of Skull after all this time. They haven't been back at all. My Uncle cleared most of Holly Cottage, but I think it still has a few of our things inside. I would love to go back."

"Seriously, after all this time? There will be some scary-looking cobwebs in that house. I will take you over there if you like? I've just got my driving license."

Eden was overcome by his offer. She so desperately wanted to experience the feeling of having a home again. "I would really like that, thank you." Eden looked away to try and maintain her composure. As she glanced over Dylan's shoulder, she noticed the coastguard had been called out to the Ferry. People were being transferred back to Cantillon.

"That's seriously weird," Dylan said as they walked through the garden and into the graveyard to get a better look. A red-faced girl ran towards them, she used the back of her hands to wipe away tears. Eden recognised her from the Carnival Noir, she was a pupil at Cantillon. The girl stopped in front of them and tried to control herself long enough to impart the only information that was important;

"There is a body in the water."

The girl's tears came once again. Dylan and Eden looked at each other, then out to sea. In the distance they could see a tiny shape being lifted from the ocean.

"A shark attack in the UK? No way, that's not possible... Is it?" Riley said as he looked up from the security monitor, whilst Dylan and Eden entered the porter cabin. Niamh was busy crouching under the desk trying to find the correct lead to connect the monitor to the computer. Scotty had his feet up on the sofa and was reading a football magazine. Amira was nowhere to be seen.

"That's what the girl said. The body was all chewed up and her leg was bitten right off," Dylan reported, as Scotty winced and rubbed his own leg.

"However unlikely it may seem, it is possible." Niamh's head popped up from under the desk for a split second before she resumed her position. "There are quite a few species found off the coast of Britain and Ireland, Basking sharks, Blue sharks, a sailing buddy of mine even spotted a Hammerhead a few months back, they are occasionally found off the British coast. They migrate." Niamh's head emerged once again, and then quickly retreated. "I read an article only last month that said Great White sharks might be occasional vagrant visitors, although I am not entirely sure what that means. The article said it's all to do with our changing weather and the fact that our conditions aren't that different to South Africa's."

Riley's face revealed his scepticism.

"Now what's this? Got it! You should have a picture now, Riley." Niamh's voice was triumphant. The monitor suddenly sprang to life; it displayed four real-time surveillance images of Cantillon. There was footage of the main entrance, the chapel, the graveyard, and the cafeteria.

"Well I, for one, don't believe it was a shark attack," Riley exclaimed as he starting typing on the keyboard. "It's just too weird, what was that poor girl doing in the water anyway?"

"Her name was Nancy and she was in John Fisher, or at least they think that it's her. She still hasn't been formally identified." Eden closed her eyes in a long blink, "I met her I think, albeit briefly. She seemed like a really sweet girl." Eden felt a chill. The horror of seeing Nancy's body dragged from the sea was still playing over in her mind.

"Maybe she smuggled some booze into the Sixth Form Ball and fell off the ferry on her way home, then a propeller got her," suggested Riley.

"How do we even know she made it to the ferry? Something or someone might have got to her on the island? We know that there was a psycho in the vicinity," Eden said looking at Dylan.

"That's just creepy Eden." Scotty screwed up his face. "I would much rather go with Riley's idea that she had a few drinks and decided to go swimming or something."

"In the pouring rain with her shoes on?" Eden challenged. "This simply can't be a coincidence. I don't want to kick up a fuss. And I certainly don't want the authorities involved in my business, but I think we owe it to Nancy to look into this ourselves."

"Well let's try and get a bit more information then," Dylan interjected, diffusing the situation. He sensed that Eden needed to be taken seriously and Scotty disagreeing with her was mistimed. "We have access to the footage from the evening. Word hasn't travelled back to security yet, so let's get a wriggle on and see whether she's caught on the campus surveillance. We can look into Eden's attack at the same time."

Niamh sat down next to Scotty, which left two small spaces for Eden and Dylan. As they squeezed on the sofa, their close proximity added yet another layer of tension to the proceedings. Riley began scanning the previous night's footage from seven o'clock. They sped through the arrival of the students at the chapel, taking note of Nancy's entrance. She was alone and arrived shortly before Eden and Niamh. Dylan had to do his utmost to maintain composure as Eden's corset lingered on screen. He caught a wink from Scotty, smiled, before feeling totally disgusted at himself for engaging in such boyish triviality when a girl had lost her life.

Riley trundled through the footage of people chatting, drinking and laughing. They watched as Dora Wilding addressed the cohort, her voice high pitched and jolty as Riley sped up the file.

"God, this is boring. When do we get to the good stuff?" Patience was not Riley's strong suit. They continued to watch the footage in silence until Eden spoke.

"I left the carnival for the beach at around ten o'clock. The whole attack must have taken about ten to fifteen minutes. So I ran into Dylan just outside the gardens, by the graveyard entrance, around 10.15pm. There is no footage of the beach, but there should be some of me leaving it and appearing just outside the graveyard and it should be coming up around... now."

Riley left the images to play in real time. Five pairs of eyes burned into the monitor. They watched for ten minutes and still nothing appeared.

"Uh, I'm going to fast-forward this." Suddenly Riley stopped in his tracks, as the grainy image of Eden came into focus. She was running through wet trees. The image quality was low, but they could all make out her expression, it was one of sheer terror. Eden kept running until she collided with Dylan, who had just entered the shot. As Eden watched the scene she noticed things she had missed the first time, like Dylan lifting her hair from her face and holding her a little longer than necessary.

"So... just *what type* of action are we looking for exactly?" Scotty's innuendo made the pair blush.

"There is clearly nothing going on here is there? Whoever was in the Banshee's Burrow with you has avoided the surveillance one way or another." Niamh interjected to save her friend from further embarrassment.

Eden felt a stab of disappointment and was beginning to wonder if she had imagined it. She had been feeling strange since arriving in Cantillon, perhaps hallucination really was another symptom.

"We should keep scanning to see if Nancy downs these so-called drinks, or goes swimming in the rain?" Dylan wanted to salvage something from the evening.

Riley began to forward the footage until they located Nancy in the chapel. She was easy to spot in her Zombie Dorothy costume. Nancy glanced around the room as if she were looking for something, then went out of the shot for a moment and returned with her bag. She made her way to the main exit.

"Right, so we have Zombie Dorothy exiting stage right at 10.43pm. Now we can try and pick her up on the graveyard camera a few minutes later." Riley trailed the images.

Eden watched Riley as he sifted through the digital footage with the confidence and experience of a professional editor. Despite his impatience, Riley was a very useful person to have at one's disposal. He seemed to have a way of getting things done.

"There! Go back Riley. There she is." Dylan stood up and pointed to a tiny image on the screen. The rest of the group watched as Nancy walked quickly through the cemetery path, which led to the harbour. She looked over her shoulder once, and continued along the path. She then went off camera.

"Is it just me, or did she look scared, as though she was being followed?" Riley said as he re-watched the scene in slow-motion.

"Hang on, yes, look there." Riley pointed with purpose at the screen. "There's a dark shadow just there." He paused the image to reveal a black smudge in the trees.

"What the hell is that? Can you zoom in?" asked Dylan as he squinted to try and make out the image.

Riley magnified the shadow, but it was still impossible to distinguish.

"Right, well we have no idea what we are looking at, and quite frankly the whole thing is now creeping even me out." Scotty shuddered. "We can't have much longer before security chuck us out. Why don't we go back and see if Nancy was caught on one of the other cameras? Surely she would have passed through Cantillon's Reception before arriving at the graveyard?"

"I'm already on it. We should see her around about now." Riley tapped the keyboard. An image of Nancy flashed up on screen. She was lit up like a beacon as she walked through the glass reception. The dark rainy night was just about visible through the glare on the windows. Nancy made her way to the front door and hesitated, the rain was pelting down. In a matter of seconds Nancy walked down the first few stone steps, she then slipped and fell out of shot.

"This is pointless, there is nothing to see." Riley sat back in his chair and rubbed his hands on his head. He stared at the screen.

"GO BACK."

Eden's voice was grave.

Her hands had begun to shake; she stood up and walked slowly towards the screen.

"Play it again in slow motion".

Riley obeyed.

Without saying a word Eden outstretched a finger and traced it along one of the windows in Cantillon's main entrance. The group leaned in.

In the reflection on the window pane was a figure. They had carefully avoided the campus surveillance, only their reflection remained. The figure had long black hair almost completely covering a bright white face. Under the hair were two black eyes, the figure seemed to move uncannily, it jolted unnaturally, its white corpse like arms outstretched as it followed Nancy down the steps.

Suddenly the security cabin door burst open.

"So what did I miss?" Amira's head appeared in the doorway, her smile faded fast.

The group sat in silence and stared at the screen.

The police arrived shortly afterwards. Scotty, Riley, Amira and Niamh were promptly sent to their respective homes and dormitories, but were told to make themselves available for interviews in the morning. Dylan and Eden were asked to remain at Cantillon to give a brief account of the events that had taken place the previous evening, as well as the footage they had viewed in the security cabin. After a few hours they were both escorted home.

Eden sank her head into the soft pillow, letting her body relax into the bed. Her legs throbbed in pain. Ever since she was a little girl she had felt this stretching pain from her toes to her hips. It only happened when she was exhausted, and tonight was no different. She went over the events of the last few days in her mind. Seeing Dylan again, the unexplained sighting from her dormitory window, the horrific incident in the Banshee's Burrow, and now a murder, most likely committed by the same person that tried to attack her earlier that evening. The very thought of it gave her chills. *Was she next on the list?* She heard the banshee's scream after all.

Eden thought back to that fateful night five years ago when everything changed. Since then she felt as though she carried something sinister with her, like she was cursed in some way. She felt like a virus that threatened to spread to innocents. She used to be so carefree and happy, but then her world fell off its axis. Now Nancy was dead, and despite all logic, she couldn't help but feel responsible.

"Are you awake?" Niamh's soft Irish accent was a welcome distraction from Eden's thoughts.

"Yes, I can't sleep,"

"How did it go with the police?"

"We spent ages going over it all. They were nice and seemed to take me seriously, I guess now we wait."

"Well it's quite the welcoming committee isn't it! New college, new home, new murder investigation. My Mam is going to have kittens when she finds out." Niamh whispered in the darkness.

"I won't be telling mine. The police tried to call them tonight, but got no answer, so at least that's something."

"Are you…" Niamh's voice trailed off. "Are you okay? I mean are you dealing with all this alright? You just don't seem to have much support."

"I don't hate my parents or anything, I just got sick of them making all my decisions. I needed some time for me, so I decided to take it here. I guess at times like this, cutting the apron strings, or burning the bloody things in my case, does leave me feeling a bit alone."

"Right, well that settles it then. I want you to look on me as your family. Whilst we are sharing this room, I am your surrogate sister."

"Being an only child, I always wanted a sister," Eden

replied. "Thank you.' It was about all she could manage without bursting into tears for the second time in two days.

Eden closed her eyes and drifted off. Her dreams were a morbid jigsaw puzzle splicing together all the horrible images from the last few days. She could hear the Rolling Stones song *Paint it Black* going round and round in her head. The most striking visual was of Nancy. She lay naked and still at the bottom of the sea, covered in seaweed. Her pale white skin was rotting. In the sores and putrefying flesh grew shells and jagged bits of coral. Crabs scuttled in and out of her wounds. Her whole body was morphing into the sea bed. A huge Great White Shark swam out of the murky water, it circled her body for a few minutes and then sank its teeth in to what was left of her, beginning with her legs.

Eden sat bolt upright in bed. It took a few moments for her to emerge from the disorientated haze of the nightmare, she glanced over at Niamh who slept peacefully. She steadied her breathing and lay back down, her own legs still throbbing in the darkness.

GENESIS

Chapter Eight

Eden woke to the smell of toast. She rubbed her eyes and glanced over to see Niamh's empty bed and wondered what had enticed her friend from the cosy sheets so early in the morning. Eden stared at the ceiling, her body felt more like sixty than sixteen. A spider had borrowed into the corner of the wall just above her pillow, she watched it for a moment. It crept along its web towards a fly that was bound there, immovable, waiting to be eaten. As she looked up at its thick furry legs, the spider fell from the web onto her chest. Without flinching, Eden scooped it up in one hand and brought it closer to her face. The spider pretended to be dead. Eden smiled, then stood on her bed and placed it back on its web, it galvanised to life and leapt happily back to its familiar home.

"Not on my watch spidey," she said plucking the fly from its silvery prison and carefully dispatching it out the window. "You can stay, but there will be no sacrificial insects whilst you are under my roof."

As Eden began to step down from her bed, she heard a cough from her doorway. Eden spun around to see Riley's wide grin.

"Sorry. Am I interrupting a beautiful moment?"

Eden scowled at him.

"I just wanted to say that Amira and I are downstairs having breakfast if you fancied some company. I see you have already made a new friend, but the offer is there."

"Thank you. After yesterday, some company would definitely be nice. If your company is all that's on offer, then I will just have to make do with that." She smiled at him cheekily.

"Hilarious. I'm glad to see that being our very own 'Final Girl' in Cantillon's horror movie hasn't affected your sense of humour."

Eden's face dropped.

"Too soon to joke about it then?"

"Yes it is, Riley, but go on, you are clearly dying to tell me. What is this 'Final Girl', then?"

"Dr Entwistle gave a lecture on it in our horror class yesterday. It's basically the last girl standing in a Slasher movie. You know the one. She's usually covered in blood, has been stabbed a couple of times, wields an axe for protection. Apparently she often has a man's name, like Sidney in *Scream*, Laurie in *Halloween*, and is extremely resourceful. So it was a compliment really."

"Apart from the stab wounds and covered in blood part." Eden was not convinced.

"Putting that bit aside, yes."

"Give me five minutes and I will be with you." Eden waited for Riley to leave so that she could change out of her pyjamas. Instead, Riley folded himself into a rocking chair, closed his eyes, and rocked frantically back and forth.

"I'm not looking!"

Eden shook her head and pulled a hooded top and jeans over her pyjamas. Once she was ready they left her dorm and locked the door. Riley grabbed her shoulders and gave her a quick squeeze as they walked down to the breakfast room.

"It's going to be fine you know." He flashed her a grin as he held the breakfast room door open, she smiled back at him, but couldn't seem to shake the sinking feeling.

Amira waved with one hand as she tucked into some blueberry pancakes with the other. She was dressed in a tight top with spaghetti straps, and tiny blue checked shorts. Her luminous warm, skin tone made Eden feel like a ghost by comparison. Amira's dark hair was gathered up in a high ponytail, a few loose curls escaped the band and framed her face. She was a vision, even in her pyjamas. She flicked through the pages of a fashion magazine. Eden got her cereal from the buffet and sat down. She was not surprised to see that Riley was eating scrambled eggs and smoked salmon. Such a costly breakfast was certainly not on the menu. Eden wondered who Riley had charmed to get his breakfast made-to-order.

"How was last night? Did the police keep you for long?" Amira asked, concerned.

"It was fine, I guess. I told them everything I knew. They weren't impressed about us busting out our best Miss Marple moves though. They told me that they wouldn't hesitate to arrest anyone who interfered with the police investigation. So I guess for now we have to be seen to leave it to the professionals."

"Well why don't we try and focus on nicer things today then, and put the whole stalker, murder thing to one side. Even if it is just for the day?" Amira smiled sheepishly at Eden. "I know this won't just go away, but I think you could use a little fun."

"Damn right, let's all bunk off and blow off some steam." Riley said literary rubbing his hands together.

Eden looked at him disapprovingly.

"This is day two of college, Riley. We can't bunk off," Amira said without even looking up from her magazine. She was clearly very used to hearing Riley's ridiculous schemes.

Eden's phone vibrated, she picked it up absentmindedly and began to read the text. As she did, a smile of excitement crept across her lips.

"Fine, well after class then?" Riley asked. "We all have Media and then we have a free period this afternoon, don't we?"

"Actually after class would be great," Eden replied typing furiously on her phone. "Amira, you have a car, right?"

"Erm, yeah I sure do. Why? Where are we going?"

"On a little adventure. It will be perfect for us. Bring snacks and sensible shoes. Shall we all meet in Amira's room after Media?"

"Sounds good," Riley confirmed.

"Oh and has anyone seen Niamh? I haven't caught sight of her this morning?"

"She hasn't been to breakfast, we have been in here since it opened. Bloody Riley and his early morning routines. Don't think this is happening every morning Riley, I will stop answering the door." Amira wagged a finger at him.

"That's odd. Well I will call her later if we don't bump into her. She might have gone to History early."

The bell sounded and Eden picked up her bowl and rushed out the door. Amira and Riley looked at each other, then down at their feet in horror. Amira wore pink flip flops, whilst Riley fashioned the latest Italian designer shoes.

"Did she just say wear sensible shoes?"

"My God that girl needs work," exclaimed Amira.

"Thank goodness she's pretty," sighed Riley.

Eden was late. She hated being late. She jogged down the corridor arranging her hair into a loose side plait, and straightening her jeans. She finally found the lecture hall and stood on tiptoes to peak into the small classroom window. Much to her dismay everyone was seated and the class had begun. She felt her cheeks burning as she quietly opened the door and slid into the seat that Amira had saved for her. Thankfully Dora Wilding didn't mention her tardiness and continued with the lecture. Riley leant forward from the row behind and whispered into her ear.

"Your flies are open. Nice frilly knickers."

For one horrendous moment Eden began to look down, and then remembered that her jeans had an elastic waistband. She fired an elbow into Riley's shin, which sent him squirming into his seat. With a victorious smile Eden sank back into her chair, ready to concentrate on the lecture, but at that moment she noticed Dylan was sitting two rows in front of her. He turned in his seat and beamed a warm smile. She had forgotten how handsome he had become. He hadn't shaved, so his dark swarthy looks seemed all the more rugged.

Eden maintained her composure and returned the gesture. Dylan turned around to face Dora, who was completely oblivious to the hive of activity that was her lecture room. Eden's eyes drifted towards a fair haired girl on Dylan's left. The girl was quite beautiful, her sun kissed skin, and naturally highlighted hair made her look European, French or Italian perhaps. She continued to whisper into Dylan's ear, and occasionally he would laugh in response. Eden knew she couldn't claim Dylan as her own, but felt the pang of jealousy nevertheless.

Eden turned her attentions to the lecture in an attempt to safeguard her feelings. Dora Wilding clicked at the computer and the words 'Citizen Journalism' flashed up on the interactive whiteboard.

"Media, and how we report the news, has transformed since the emergence of social media technologies. The twenty-first century has become dominated by developments in personal technologies. There is now a culture of availability, where there is no 'switch off'. Our whole lives are being narrated online. Our social media profiles are constantly changing public diaries that include the most intimate details of our daily lives. With the multitude of Citizen Journalism sites available to us we are now able to report the news from our bedrooms, classrooms, offices."

Eden was momentarily drawn into Dora's lecture. Despite her odd persona, she was a compelling speaker. As Eden continued to listen, once again her eyes fell on the fair-haired girl next to Dylan. She tried to pull them away, but as she did a strange thing happened. The girl turned and stared straight back at her. Mortified, Eden averted her eyes, but the girl didn't. Several seconds past, but the girl's eyes continued to bore into Eden. Her face was expressionless, she neither frowned or smiled, she simply stared unashamedly at Eden. Eventually, much to Eden's relief, her gaze was interrupted when Dora handed her the homework assignment. But Eden needed to know - who was this strange girl that had become Dylan's muse?

"So to the first assignment of the year," Dora continued. "Citizen Journalism, or what one might call amateur news reporting, is now commonplace. Over the next two weeks you are required to report a local news story in the form of an online blog. The college have created their own virtual learning environment where these can be uploaded, and you are encouraged to read each other's journals. The remainder of the session will now continue in the library where you can begin to explore the stories that you want to tell. But before we leave, I will divide you into groups."

Dora quickly went around the room and allotted study groups. Eden watched as Dylan was put with Scotty and the fair haired girl, whilst she was with Riley and Amira. With that, the class erupted into noise. People stood up, packed their bags, and started to make their way to the library. As Eden queued to leave the lecture hall, she found herself next to Dylan.

"I was late, too. I think we have a pretty good excuse considering."

"Agreed." Eden's voice sounded a little icier than she had intended.

"Eden, this is Oregan. We met in Film yesterday. Oregan is another horror geek, I'm afraid." Dylan's attempt at humour was quite transparent. Eden could tell that he was feeling as awkward as she was.

"Hi," Eden managed to force her lips to say the word. Oregan responded with only a half-smile, before turning her back on Eden completely, and speaking exclusively to Dylan.

"Dylan, I have those tickets for the weekend, so I will drop them over to you later this evening if you like?" Oregan's smouldering eyes seemed to have a magnetic hold on him.

Eden felt a tightening in her chest. *Were they going on a date?* Eden stood next to them feeling ridiculous, until Scotty emerged from the crowd. He immediately extended a hand and managed to pluck her back to reality.

"Eden, my darling, how are you doing? What a day it was yesterday, come walk and talk with me."

Eden could have kissed him, not in a romantic sense, although his impressive looks would be difficult for most girls to ignore, but to thank him, she was in his debt. Eden took his outstretched arm and the pair wandered to the library together. His big bold voice and expressive hands made Eden feel tiny. She laughed the entire journey, and for a few moments forgot about Oregan. Once they arrived in the library, Eden's group were assigned to the computer next to Dylan, Oregan and Scotty. Eden took a deep breath, the next couple of hours were going to be difficult.

"So who was the hot Goth?" Riley asked as he lounged across the back seat of Amira's Jeep.

"Have some sensitivity, Riley, for Christ sake," Amira scorned him in the rear view mirror.

"Her name is Oregan." Eden stared out of the passenger seat window as the rain speckled on the glass.

"She was frosty as hell. Sorry, I am mixing my metaphors, but you know what I mean. I think she hated you a little bit Eden."

"Yes, thank you Riley, I got that."

Amira took a red finger-nailed hand from the steering wheel and squeezed Eden's shoulder. Unlike Riley, Amira picked up on Eden's melancholy mood, and understood the source. "She and Dylan met in Film yesterday, they were both geeking out about some horror director. There is nothing in it, I am sure of it."

"Thanks, Amira. I wouldn't be so sure, though. They are going out together over the weekend. But anyway, I don't even have a right to be upset, so let's move on. Sorry for the wallowing. Bad mood over."

"So, this isn't going to be like that film *Twister* is it? I don't want to end up being swept away in a tornado." Riley helped himself to a packet of sweets from Amira's bag.

"No, you will be quite safe Riley, I promise. Storm chasing is only dangerous if you chase weather without an exit strategy. We won't enter the storm; we will watch it from a safe distance. The chances are it's out to sea anyway."

Amira crunched the gear stick into fourth.

"Ouch," Riley winced.

Amira eyed him again in the rear-view mirror. Riley had his feet up on the seat and was lying down. "Seriously Riley, I passed my test a week ago. I would wear a seatbelt if I were you." Riley looked back at Amira and revealed that despite his ridiculous position, he had somehow still managed to wear his seatbelt.

"See!" Riley quipped. "Eden, besides the rain it doesn't look particularly stormy, what exactly are we looking for?"

Eden checked that her camera had a full battery and opened an app on her phone. "Well, first off we are looking for instability in the atmosphere. But we can skip that bit as both the weather forecast and my online friends have already forecast a storm and identified the area. I will get five minute updates on my app, but until I get a bit more knowledgeable about Cantillon and Skull geography, I won't be able to 'read the sky' as weather watchers say. I still have loads to learn, but to answer your question, we are looking for fast moving cumulous clouds." Eden turned around to see that Riley had fallen asleep.

"Charming."

"I am interested, Eden. His attention span is like a gnat, I am afraid."

In the distance Eden saw a murky grey throbbing cloud.

"There," Eden was suddenly animated. "Follow that if you can." Eden's phone continued to chime with social media alerts. "Take Devon Street."

The storm was nearly upon them, rain pelted down on the windscreen so loudly that Riley began to stir. The car swerved around a sharp corner, and Eden saw what she was looking for.

The sky was black. The ocean spray fused into storm clouds that rotated over the ocean, in the distance a bolt of lightning penetrated deep into the crashing waves. For a moment the sky lit up like a doorway to another realm, and then it vanished, and darkness prevailed.

"A supercell," Eden said, in awe.

"A what, now?" Amira shouted over the hail stones.

"A supercell, storms are like weather in a box, supercells rotate. Look at the way it's twisting and turning." Eden decided that there was not going to be a better spot. "You two stay in the car, I am going to get some footage of this."

"Seriously, you expect us to stay in a metal box when there is lightning around? Did I do something to you?" Riley rubbed his eyes and slowly sat up.

"It's a Faraday cage, you will be fine." Eden pulled on her raincoat.

"A Faraday what?"

"A Faraday cage. It's the laws of physics. If you are in a cage or a metal structure and get struck by lightning the charge will go around you."

Amira and Riley exchanged worried glances.

"I will be back in a few minutes. Trust me, it will be fine."

Amira and Riley watched as Eden put up her hood and headed out into the storm with no hesitation. Eden rigged up her photographic equipment as the hailstones fell around her and gusts of wind blew her from side to side.

"She is a crazy person!" Riley noted, seeing a marked change in his usually cautious friend.

"I'm going to film her in case we need to use it as evidence when she washes up on the beach!" Riley pulled out his phone and began to video Eden. As Riley watched the live footage, his face began to take on a paler tone than usual.

"No that can't be." Riley kept looking from the camera to Eden. "Jesus. We need to call her back. Get her inside the car, NOW!"

Riley was so scarcely serious, the hairs on Amira's neck began to prickle.

"Why? What the hell's going on? Riley, you are scaring

me." Amira grabbed the camera phone from Riley, and looked at the image of Eden. Through the lens Amira saw Eden standing next to her camera and tripod in the lashing rain as she filmed the storm. But every time Eden moved, hundreds of tiny electrical charges bounced off her body up into the sky. Through the camera lens the bolts of electricity made Eden look like she was being electrocuted, but miraculously she felt no pain. It was as though she was actually channelling the weather.

Amira threw down the phone and looked at Eden, but the charges had disappeared.

"So those weird wiggly white lines that look like lightning are only visible through a camera lens? What the hell are they?"

"I'm guessing they create some kind of portal for lightning to travel through, which means right now she's a sitting target. All it takes is for lightning to travel down one of those avenues and she's all Carol Anne from *Poltergeist*." Riley bit his lip. "Urgh! Why couldn't we've just got some booze and watched a trashy movie. I can't just sit back and do nothing. These bloody outdoorsy types, they will kill us all in the end."

Amira snatched up the phone once again and watched, powerless, as Riley entered the shot. His broad shoulders lifted Eden clear off the ground and carried her back into the car.

"Your storm chasing days are over." Riley's face was grave, for a moment he was genuinely frightening.

Eden didn't say a word, she just picked up Riley's phone and replayed the footage. She watched in horror as her body was transformed into a mass of electrical currents, charges bounced off her flesh like flames. The Jeep trundled its way down the hill, bolts of lightning lit up the sky behind them.

Chapter Nine

The spider was back. Eden stretched out her arms and pulled the duvet back from her bed. Her bones cracked as she stood up and removed the spider's latest winged hostage, a small brown and white moth. She looked at the crumpled little creature.

"You look like I feel." Eden felt as though she had just returned from a marathon, not eight hours of sleep. As Eden made her way to her ensuite bathroom, she noticed that her breakfast had been neatly arranged on the bedside table, there was an accompanying note with the words 'eat me' inscribed.

E

Thanks for your call yesterday. Leviathan and I went fishing. See you after class tonight for chocolate and a catch up. Hope you are okay.
N

Eden sank into the rocking chair and pulled a blanket over her legs. The ocean glistened as the boiling tea stung her lips. Usually Eden loved breakfast, especially if she had some time to herself. There was something about the morning sun, the quiet, the calm, the anticipation of what the day may bring, that had always appealed to her. But this morning was different. Eden couldn't shake the sick feeling in the pit of her stomach. She couldn't keep the image of Nancy's tiny corpse being dragged out of the sea from her mind. Yesterday's wake-up call at the storm chase left her feeling even more anxious.

Eden had worked into the night to try and get to the

bottom of the horrifying images she had watched on Riley's phone. From her previous experience of storms, she understood enough about lightning to know that it was very possible for a human being to send what was called 'an upward streamer' into the sky. She also knew that whilst it may have looked as though surges of electricity were bouncing off her flesh, other forces had to be present to create an actual lightning bolt. These upward streamers were simply pathways that lightning *could* travel down. However, what Eden couldn't figure out, and what was missing from all the research she had read, was why her entire body was covered in hundreds of these streamers. From the images she had scoured on the internet, she realised that the majority of cases were of a single streamer. Eden wondered what on earth had caused so many of them to gravitate to her. It seemed simply impossible. *Was there something terribly wrong with her?* Eden's mind began to wander back to that dark place in her memories that she was constantly battling to evade. She closed her eyes tight and locked the memory of that night out of her mind, the way she had done so many times before.

Since returning to Cantillon, Eden had been reminded of her own mortality on two separate, equally terrifying, occasions. Right now she couldn't get the Banshee's scream out of her head. *Was she going to make it through the first week of college?* There was a killer at large who, in all likelihood, wanted to make Eden their next target. She had so many questions that needed answers. *Who or what was preying on her and for what purpose? Why was Nancy killed and mutilated? Does this link back to that fateful night?*

Eden rubbed her eyes and cupped her face in her hands. Today was not a good day to be alone. She needed to be with Dylan. With that, she picked up her phone.

After a long shower that rejuvenated her achy limbs, Eden began the arduous process of beautification. She spent ten minutes looking blankly at her wardrobe, before finally selecting some black jeans, and a teal off-the-shoulder T-shirt, which she teamed with a chunky silver necklace. Finally she was ready and rushed out the door, leaving her bedroom floor covered with hair straighteners, make-up brushes, and tubes of foundation. She hoped that Niamh would be late home tonight so Eden would have a chance to clean up.

At eleven o'clock Eden approached Dylan's driveway ready for their outing to Holly Cottage. The Blake residence had scarcely changed since they were children, but Eden was surprised to see how small it was. As a child everything seems so big and grand. The house was full of character. It was a wood construction that had been painted white, with pale blue shutters. The whole structure was suspended on stilts, with a generous veranda that contained three rocking chairs. Eden remembered spending many summers evenings having barbecues on the veranda. As the evenings drew in, Dylan and Eden would practice being as quiet as mice to avoid drawing attention to their impending bedtime. Sometimes they would crawl under the veranda stairs and hide from their parents. It was only when they heard the panic in the grown-up's voices that they emerged from their hidey-hole, covered in dirt and cobwebs.

Eden pulled back the iron knocker, and a familiar face appeared behind the door.

"Eden, my goodness, how absolutely wonderful to see you.' Judy hugged Eden tightly. Dylan's mother was just as Eden had remembered. Her lovely, kind face was simply beaming, Eden couldn't believe that Dylan's father could bear to leave such a woman. Eden followed Judy into the house and settled down on the sofa in the living room, where she was instantly overcome with feelings of nostalgia. The pictures that hung on the walls of Dylan and Beth, the little ornaments of Corgi dogs that sat on the fireplace, the smell of coffee and freshly washed clothes, all transported her back to when she was ten years old. Eden felt like she had come home for the first time in years. Everything in her life was so new, so lacking in history, but these walls were full of memories.

"You are looking so well Eden. You have grown into a beautiful young woman."

Eden blushed a little, but was delighted this morning's getting-ready-process hadn't gone unnoticed.

"How are your Mum and Dad?" There was something about the awkward manner in which Judy asked that made Eden desperately look for a distraction. She couldn't risk another line of questioning about the Hollows' sudden departure from Skull. Eden stood up and began to browse the photographs on the mantel piece. She picked up a silver frame containing a picture of herself, Dylan, and Beth; they were laughing as they buried Judy in the sand. Their bodies looked tiny in their swimsuits.

"Fine, thanks," Eden replied quickly as she tapped a finger at the photograph. "This brings back memories."

Judy leapt up to share in the sentimentality. "It rained all day long, but it didn't spoil a thing. Look at Beth's face. She loved nothing more than building sand castles on the beach. How the time flies. That was ten years ago."

Eden looked into Judy's face and noticed that she may not be quite as youthful and bubbly as she first appeared. Time takes its toll on everyone, she thought. At that moment, the door swung open and Dylan walked into his living room, Converse trainers in hand. His hair was wet from the shower.

"Morning, ladies."

Judy smiled at him, whilst Eden made a face as she tapped her watch. She couldn't believe that he had only just torn himself away from his duvet. Judy picked up the local paper and glanced at the headline.

Judy paused. "The news about that poor girl is just so very sad."

Eden thought she saw a tear glisten at the corner of Judy's eye.

"How absolutely awful to be taken like that, and for you to get caught up in the middle of it. Eden, you must have been terrified. Well, there is always a bed for you in this house. Since Dylan"'s father left, we have become terribly relaxed, so whenever you fancy a sleepover or just a little company don't hesitate to call. We would love to have you."

"Thank you," Eden replied respectfully. "I have a very nice roommate at Cantillon, but I will keep that in mind."

Judy's kind eyes were fixed on Eden. "You know Beth would have loved to have seen you."

Dylan tied his shoelaces, jumped up and kissed his mother on the head. "Sorry, Mum. We really must be off now. Eden will come over another time for a proper chat." And with that they were out the door in seconds.

"Sorry about Mum. She has become rather emotional in her old age. She always looked on you as a second daughter."

Eden smiled. Judy had been so good to her. Dylan pulled his car keys from his pocket and made his way over to the Black Volkswagen Golf.

Eden laid a hand on his arm. "If it's okay with you, I thought we could walk."

"Let's take the scenic route." Dylan grinned.

Eden and Dylan walked along the beach towards Willow Woods. Eden looked across the white sand. She could just about make out the spot where the photograph on Judy's mantel had been taken all those years ago. Eden loved beaches, the salty smell, the warm sand on her skin, but, most of all, she loved the fact they were so primitive. Beaches were constant, they never changed, they were as nature intended.

As they walked away from the beach and further into the forest, Eden could see Holly Cottage's roof poking out amongst the trees. They meandered through the clearing. Huge weeping willows dwarfed them overhead. The morning dew dripped from the leaves and glistened as the sun broke through the branches. They unwittingly interrupted two rabbits, which bolted off into the distance.

"Look, do you remember this?" Dylan tied two willow tree branches together and created a swing. "Ladies first."

"Okay, but if I end up in the stream, I am not going to take it well!" Eden lifted herself into the swing and Dylan pulled it back ready to propel her over the water. "Ready?"

"I guess." Eden said sceptically.

Dylan let go of the branch and Eden swung all the way across the pond, screaming as she gained momentum.

"My bad. I forgot that it was the stopping bit that we could never seem to master," Dylan called after her.

"Now would be a good time to learn then, and fast," Eden yelled.

With that, Dylan waited for Eden to swing towards him. He held out his arms and grabbed her around the waist, lifting her clear of the swing in one easy motion. She held on to him until everything stopped spinning and for a moment they stood statically in a lingering embrace.

"Erm, ouch," Dylan said as Eden slapped his arm. "People seriously need to stop hitting me."

"Thanks for that!"

"I saved you, didn"t I?"

"You were the one who made the swing and pushed me in the first place!"

"Yes, that is all true. But still, I absolutely made up for it, in an entirely chivalrous manner I might add."

"Hmmm." Eden would not give him the satisfaction of her agreement.

"You, my dear, need to try and stop crashing into me. That is twice now. If you want a hug, just ask."

"You are impossible. Don't flatter yourself."

Dylan and Eden had become so animated by their discussion that they had failed to notice their arrival at Holly Cottage. Eden's face dropped as she took in her surroundings.

The bushes had become overgrown and wild. The climbing frame that she used to play on as a child was now completely covered with foliage. The house itself was dilapidated, with paint peeling off the outside walls, windows boarded, and various bits of rubbish, including a mattress and an inflatable paddling pool, were strewn in the garden. It was a dump. Disappointment washed over her. Holly Cottage looked more like a crime scene than her childhood home.

Eden had such high hopes for this moment. Ever since she was ripped from her bed five years ago, she had taken herself back to the last place that she had felt safe. All those nights she spent alone in Worcestershire, lying awake in the dark, were made fractionally more bearable when she pictured Holly Cottage. On her worst nights she would picture every part of Holly Cottage in her mind. It was calming and made her feel cosy. But the reality fell very short of the nostalgic fantasy. The pair walked carefully up the stone steps to the front door, each step was covered in moss, their feet threatened to slide off at any minute. Eden opened the door the same way she had done as a child. She slid her slender arm through the letterbox and bent her elbow so that she could reach the inside lock. The door clicked open.

Dylan tried to lighten the atmosphere. "I can't believe you can still do that." He could read the disappointment on her face, and wanted to make it better for her, but he realised that this was beyond him, the moment was all hers. He had to be a bystander.

They stood in the large entrance hall. As the sun beat through the cracks, the silvery cobwebs sparkled. The fireplace that had at one point been so grand, the heart of the house, was now covered in pigeon feathers and soot. It looked meagre by comparison. Eden walked over to it and ran a finger across the mantel, dust particles permeated the air. The entrance hall contained an impressive winding staircase and four heavy set oak doors, each leading to a different part of the house; the kitchen, the bathroom, the library, and the lounge. Dylan watched Eden move around her once familiar belongings like a ghost, until he could take it no more.

"Eden, I think I might sit in the library and give you a little time to absorb it all."

Eden scarcely heard him speak.

Dylan walked over to her and placed one hand on her shoulder, her eyes didn't meet his, they just glazed over and continued to stare blankly into the room as though in a trance. "I am in here if you need me."

Eden still made no sound.

"Eden, are you sure you are okay? You look a bit off colour all of a sudden?"

"Yes, I'm fine, thank you. I will call if I need you." Eden was already walking robotically up the staircase, as though there was something up there, drawing her in.

Dylan opened the door to the library, but it got stuck on something the other side. As Dylan pushed harder and manoeuvred his way into the next room, he saw a large bag of clothes and a number of other personal items that looked out of place in the cottage. They were too new, and too clean. There was a hairbrush, an overnight bag, some make-up, amongst other things. Squatters, Dylan thought. He decided he would not mention it to Eden. It was another detail that might push her over the edge. He picked up the bag and moved it into a dark corner where it would go undetected. Dylan sank into Charles Hollow's leather chair and put his feet up on the desk. For a moment he enjoyed the novelty of sitting at Eden's father's writing desk. As children Dylan and Eden were both forbidden from stepping foot in the library. Dylan had always found Charles to be a scary, powerful man and never dared to go against his will. On the desk sat a little bouncy ball in the shape of a globe. Dylan picked it up and began to throw it against the wall. The rhythmic bouncing echoed through the house and up the stairs to Eden.

Eden stood at the top of the stairs. The house was just as they left it that night five years ago. She couldn't believe how much her parents had left behind. Eden walked a few feet and stood outside her bedroom door, it was closed. She took a deep breath and braced herself. Her last moments in the house were spent in this very room, and they had changed her forever.

Dylan continued to bounce the ball against the wall. He stretched back in the leather chair, momentarily losing balance as the seat adjusted. The ball flew out of his hand and hit the adjoining wall. As the ball impacted on the wall, it made a strange echoey sound; the wall had a hollow panel. Dylan threw the ball again and heard the same cavernous echo. Dylan got out of his chair and climbed onto the desk, his curiosity getting the better of him. He felt around for the trigger to open the compartment. In old movies secret compartments were usually opened by pushing a fake book in a bookcase or by lifting a leaver under a desk. He scanned the library shelves but nothing seemed out of place. He stepped down and felt under the desk but there were no concealed leavers. Dylan thought for a moment. 'Where are you?'

Dylan glanced around the room. As he did so, Dylan noticed a small box of matches positioned in the far right hand corner of the desk. He smiled and wondered if he could possibly be that lucky. He struck the match against the flint provided on the desk, and held the flame against a tiny thermostat that was attached to it. The flame began to curl around the tips of his fingers, but he gritted his teeth and continued. As the thermostat heated up it changed colour and the panel popped open. Dylan could hardly believe it. "Thank you Mum and your rubbish detective dramas." Judy had a penchant for trashy American murder mysteries, and Dylan had recently been subjected to an old episode of *Murder She Wrote* where the killer employed a similar contraption. Dylan checked outside the library door to make sure there was no sign of Eden; he heard the floorboards creak above him.

Dylan hesitated. He knew that he shouldn't look inside the panel, his morals told him that he should allow Eden's father his privacy, but he wanted to know more about their strange disappearance. How could he protect Eden if he didn't understand the situation, after all knowledge is power. Eden needed him. She was so different now, broken. He reached into the small compartment and pulled out the contents. There were some photographs, an odd-looking antique made from pearl and some kind of metal, and a stack of papers and letters. He rifled through the top papers and there was nothing of interest, just some bills and bank statements. Then, underneath an old mortgage statement, a letter caught his eye. He opened it and began to read. Dylan stared at the paper, his hands began to shake.

Eden folded her fingers around the door knob and pushed the door open. Her bed was unmade; the duvet was strewn untidily all over the mattress. The floor was covered in shattered ornaments and toys. The wooden bookcase was broken and had splintered all over the room. The blood had been cleared away, but that was all. A wave of nausea came over her, her eyes lost their ability to focus. She flopped to her knees, as her whole body went cold. She put her head to the ground and doubled over as an excruciating pain in the pit of her stomach pulsated through every muscle, it blinded her. She lay in the same spot that she fell into five years ago, it was like she was stuck in a perpetual groundhog day. And then his panic-stricken face came into view. He came closer, she felt his strong arms underneath her, holding her. Then everything went black.

Chapter Ten

"Eden, Eden do you know where you are?" The voice wasn't familiar.

Eden opened her stinging eyes. Her head felt as though all her brain matter had come loose and was banging around in her skull. After a few moments the fog lifted, and she slowly sat up. Eden looked down to see that she was wearing a blue hospital gown; the strong odour of disinfectant filled the room. A tall, thick set man with a wild grey mane and disturbingly long nasal hair stood at her bedside. He introduced himself as Dr Lister, a Registrar, and began his inquisition.

"Eden, you are in St Peter's Infirmary. Do you know what day it is?"

"Yes. It's Wednesday 10th September."

Lister"s eyes narrowed. He didn't expect his patient to be so precise after such an episode.

"Yes, that is accurate, Eden. Now, can you remember what happened to you earlier today?"

"I'm sorry, this is probably a huge waste of your time. I'm sure I will be fine now. I was okay one minute and the next I felt a pain in my stomach. My whole body seemed to just give up on me. I must have fainted or something. I have been feeling a bit weak for a while. I thought it might be flu or tiredness as my sleeping has been quite erratic."

Lister's well-worn eyes fixed on Eden's like magnets. She was afraid to look away. He was incredibly intense.

"It would be preferable if you leave the diagnosis to us Eden." Lister continued his questioning, he sat completely still, he didn't move his hands, or nod his head as he spoke. Eden imagined his face would crack if he even attempted a smile. Lister asked Eden about drugs and alcohol consumption, and whether she had been abroad recently. He even asked her if she could be pregnant, at which point Eden's cheeks became engulfed in flames of embarrassment. Lister then informed Eden that she would be kept in for observation. The nurse would be doing her rounds shortly. After providing some blood and urine samples, Eden would then be moved to a ward.

A few hours later, two men in blue uniforms wheeled Eden's bed to her residence for the night. Due to a shortage of space on the ward, she was given a private room. Eden settled in for the evening. She switched on the television but the channels offered either soap operas or reality TV, both of which Eden couldn't abide. She had no belongings with her, no phone or computer, and there were no books on the shelves. Eden couldn't believe how difficult it was to lie down and just do nothing. She needed stimulation of some sort or she would go out of her mind. One hour in hospital felt like an entire day in the outside world. This was Eden's first experience of such places, and hopefully she would only be there for one night.

Eden switched the television back on and settled on *House*, a hospital drama series. She watched as the cast of beautiful, youthful doctors argued over the diagnosis of a man whose only ailment was that he couldn't stop laughing. They walked around beautifully lit, freshly painted corridors, carrying *Starbucks* cups. Eden noticed water features, and decorative glass wall dividers in the background of the shot. She glanced around her own room with its stark lighting, brown and yellow walls, and blue spotted curtains. Lister was certainly a very different looking individual to Dr House, although they shared a brash, bordering on rude, bedside manner. She heard someone wrap their fingers against the window. Judy and Dylan appeared in the doorway carrying flowers, magazines, and an overnight bag. Eden attempted to curtail her excitement as they walked in and sat on the little brown chairs.

"My darling, how are you?" Judy walked over to her, arms outstretched, and gave her a sympathetic squeeze.

"They have taken good care of me, but I am going out of my mind with boredom already."

"What on earth happened to you? Dylan, poor love, was white as a sheet when he came home to get the car. He had been in the waiting room most of the day. He only popped back to fetch the car so he could drive over to your dorm and pick up an overnight bag."

"Mum." Dylan was clearly embarrassed by Judy's disclosure.

Eden cringed at the thought of him going through her clothes and private things. She hoped Niamh had packed the bag. She would much rather think of Niamh riffling through her granny knickers and sports bras than Dylan.

"Thank you so much Dylan. I'm sorry I gave you a fright. I feel much better now. Was Niamh home at all?" Eden hoped she was being subtle.

"Yes, she was. She said to tell you she will be over later."

Eden thought his face seemed more solemn than usual. At first she put it down to concern, but wondered if something else had upset him.

"I am glad you feel better."

Judy went on to ask more about Eden's condition and precisely what Lister had discussed. "Your parents have been called, but I am afraid we couldn't get through to them. We left a message on your father's voicemail. I hope I didn't sound too dramatic."

"I totally forgot. They are away at the moment. I will call them again later." Eden remembered that her parents were on holiday in Scotland, visiting her uncle. She really didn't want her parents to return to the very place they clearly couldn't wait to leave, but there was no way they would abandon her whilst she was in hospital and simply continue with their holiday. She would call them as soon as Judy and Dylan left, and play down the whole situation.

Even if it meant telling a few white lies, she would make sure that they didn't fly back.

Judy continued to take care of Eden's every need, from propping pillows, to arranging her towels. She even offered to take her to the toilet, to which Eden drew the line. Amidst Judy's constant chattering and fussing, which was a welcome distraction for Eden, Dylan seemed comparatively quiet and distant. She wanted to ask him if he was okay, but couldn't find the words. As Judy and Dylan left he kissed Eden's cheek, and she whispered the words 'thank you' into his ear, but his eyes looked blankly at the floor. He offered her a meagre half smile, and left. She kept her eyes on him as he walked down the corridor, she willed his head to turn, right up to the moment he disappeared out the double doors.

Eden wanted today to be over. She made the call to her parents then sank her head into the crunchy brown pillow. To her surprise, sleep came immediately, a deep, dreamless sleep.

Dylan's eyes burned into the letter. He couldn't remember how many times he had read it. He wished he had never found it. This morning everything was full of potential, and now everything had become tangled and warped. He didn't know if Eden remembered what she had said to him, as she lay limp and lifeless, cradled in his arms. But if she did remember, she had an excellent poker face. He tried to shake it off, to rationalise it as part of her strange mental episode, the speech of someone with diminished responsibility. But when he looked into her eyes, he knew she had never spoken a truer word, it would stay with him forever. They were cold eyes. Long gone was their sparkle, and the zest for life that used to twinkle within them. He could still picture her lips curling around the words.

"I will never be yours."

And so it was over as quickly as it started. When she arrived she came hurtling out of the darkness and now she had rescinded back into it. It would be so easy for him to let his pride, his hurt, his sadness consume him, and to forget about the letter, but he knew that Eden deserved more than that. He still wanted to be in her life, in whatever capacity she would accept. Frustration, fear, anxiety, all percolated in his mind as he re-read the letter one more time.

Mrs M. J. Hollow
The Ridge
One Brocketts Way
Shepperton
Middlesex

4th June 1999
Dearest Charles,

I write to you for the fourth time, as I have yet to receive a response. I hope that by now you and Delia have come to your senses about the child. I say this as a mother, who is thinking of her son's best interests, don't throw your life away for someone else's mistake. You know nothing about the child's heritage, her background. You do not yet know what it means to have a child, to love them completely, to care for them every moment of their lives. I fear that one day someone will come for her and your life will be ruined. You will bring shame on your family and Delia's heart will be broken.

If you cannot find it in your heart to reply to my correspondence, then at least consider these words. They are written with you in mind.

All my love, always
Mother

What was he going to do about the contents? He couldn't tell Eden, not yet. He must establish the truth before he could consider exposing her to such heartache. The letter turned everything on its head, it called her whole life history, her blood line, into question. Who was her real father? He needed to do some digging, and he would start with his own mother.

At that moment Beth poked her head around his door. Her thick, dark pigtails swished on her shoulders as she glided into his room, even her walk breathed energy into those who had the pleasure to witness it. Dylan stuffed the letter under his thigh as he sat on the sofa. Beth had a habit of appearing whenever he was feeling down, and needed someone to just listen. She smiled at him and put her arm around his shoulders, she leaned her head on his for just a few moments.

"Eden?"

"Afraid so."

"Oh, DJ. Here we go again."

Judy's mouth curled into an awkward half smile. The letter sat on the dining room table next to the dinner plates, the remnants of spaghetti bolognese was still visible. Judy picked up the paper for the second time, and read it once again. She sat silently for a few moments, not knowing how to answer her son.

"Mum, I understand that you don't want to betray confidences, and I know that you might think that it would be better for Eden if I just left matters alone. To be honest I am not even sure whether I am going to tell her myself – but please, what do you know? You and Delia were very tight back then, you must know something."

"Dylan, I do think that some things are better left unsaid, darling. It's not our business, and she won't thank you. You shouldn't have poked around in matters that don't concern you."

Frustrated, Dylan tried a different tactic. "What if it had been me, or Beth? Would we deserve to know that Dad wasn't our real Dad? Surely you can see that something seriously wrong has gone on in that house? Someone needs to look after her."

"Dylan, there is more to being a father than just biology. It was Charles that raised her and cared for her. He's her *real* father, as you say. It takes two minutes to make a baby, but a lifetime to raise one. This is complex and I don't know if you can fully comprehend the extent of this situation at your age."

"Please don't patronise me, Mum. I appreciate that Charles has done a lot for her, but I think that you have lost sight of what's happening here. Eden has been deceived her entire life. It's not for anyone else to decide for her, she deserves to know the truth about something so fundamental to her whole existence." Dylan made a compelling argument.

Judy looked at him, at the man he had become. She felt caught between pride and frustration. "I will tell you this, there is much more to this than you know. Can you give me a couple of days to think it over? Then, once I have carefully considered the facts, I will tell you what you need."

As much as Dylan wanted to push his mother, he respected her judgement and didn't want to upset her. He could wait.

Judy got up from the dinner table and cleared away the dishes in silence. Dylan watched as she loaded the plates in the dishwasher. She looked ten years older.

Chapter Eleven

It was pitch black. Eden couldn't sleep. She reached over to her bedside table and switched on her nightlight. The latest copy of *The Skull Herald* sat on the chair next to her bed. She picked it up and rolled her eyes as she read the front-page headline, 'Wizard of Oz Shark Attack'. Whilst the sensationalist headline took up the majority of the column space, the article itself was comparatively brief and under-reported.

Wizard of Oz Shark Attack

The body of Nancy Grange, a sixteen year old budding gymnast from Northern Skull, was recovered by police off the coast of Cantillon on Wednesday. The young woman's remains were discovered earlier that afternoon by passengers on the Seaford Ferry crossing from Cantillon to Skull. Nancy had been reported missing since the previous evening and was last seen wearing a Dorothy Gale fancy dress costume from the Wizard of Oz. Few details have been released by police concerning the nature of the incident, but early sources have linked the injuries to an alleged shark attack. If the sources prove to be correct, this will be the first shark attack fatality in British waters. Experts have been notified and are currently scrutinising the evidence. Local beaches will remain open, but swimmers are encouraged to stay vigilant and to avoid swimming in deep water.

Eden continued to read the remainder of the article, she let out a groan as she turned the page to see a double page spread entitled 'UK's Jaws', which comprised of gratuitous, insensitive shock stories related to shark attacks. Articles ranged from 'Shark Victim Gives Advice on How to Stay Alive,' with images of a woman's shark attack injuries, to 'Is it Safe to Go in the Water: Shark Encounters off the British Isles,' which listed every registered shark encounter from 1845. Eden found it incredible that readers would even consider the possibility of a shark attack.

"Skull-on-Sea is hardly Amity Island," Eden said aloud as she shook her head. She flicked through the subsequent six pages of what she considered to be ridiculous scare mongering rubbish. One article even included an interview with a local fisherman who had chartered a boat to hunt 'the Beast.'

Eden knew that there was something far more dangerous and premeditated behind the attack, than a mere shark. She tried to stop her mind from thinking about the mass of dripping dark hair, and that evil white face, but it was constantly tapping away at her brain. She felt as though she was missing something painfully obvious. There were so many odd things about the murder. She wondered why Nancy's leg had been severed. Eden initially presumed that Nancy had received the injuries post-mortem, after her body had been dumped in the sea, various sea creatures would have feasted on the flesh without question. But the article states that her leg had been severed and that Nancy died from her injuries, and this is what implicated a shark attack. But Eden knew that a shark was not the predator in question. But why would someone sever Nancy's leg? Was it not enough to abduct someone and drown them? But to butcher her in this way was just too grisly a demise. Was it some warped reference to the *Wizard of OZ* and the ruby slippers? It seemed so far-fetched, what would motivate someone to do such a thing?

Eden felt sick.

She needed to stop thinking about Nancy and get some sleep. She folded the paper and placed it on her nightstand, and switched off her night light. Riley, Amira, and Niamh would be visiting in the morning, she could talk it over with them. Hopefully the hospital would sign her release forms in the afternoon, and she could begin her convalescence in Cantillon. Eden closed her eyes and conjured Holly Cottage in her mind. Not the house that she entered hours earlier, but the home that she lived in as a little girl. She pictured the snails she would pluck from the reeds and the little stone wall with its loose slabs that she used to lift up and discover a whole world of insects. The smell of cut grass, the soft wet lawn under her feet and the sound of the rippling water as she skipped stones on the lake. Gradually the thoughts left her mind and she drifted into sleep.

Eden opened her eyes; it was still dark. She pulled her sheets around her. She was freezing. The cold had woken her. She smelled something, a rancid odour, a pungent metallic stench that she recognised, but couldn't quite place. She felt for her nightlight, but it was no longer there. Then, she remembered where she had smelt it before, it was a Year Nine Science class when she dissected a pig's kidney.

It was the smell of blood.

Her breath made a mist as she exhaled. She was no longer in her private room. She wasn't sure how she got here, but she knew that there was only one place she could be: the morgue.

As her eyes began to adjust and make out the shapes of the room, she felt a presence next to her. She turned her head slowly, to see the figure that lay on the adjoining table.

Expressionless eyes looked back at her.

Pale white skin with mottled patches of green and blue lay exposed on the table.

A deep Y-shaped incision ran from her shoulder blades to her naked lower sternum.

Her whole body looked as though it had been feasted on by something. There were chunks ripped out and bruises in the shape of bite marks where teeth hadn't quite managed to break the skin but had gripped the flesh for some time.

It was Nancy.

Eden wondered why someone would bring her here.

What was she supposed to see? Were they trying to scare her?

Eden noticed how heavy Nancy's body looked lying on the cold, white slab. It was as if having a soul made a person lighter somehow. Eden knew she should have felt fear. Others in her situation may have screamed or vomited, but all Eden felt was sadness and a sense of loss.

Eden slipped out of bed and walked over to Nancy. For a moment she forgot her own weakness and fell to the ground, but quickly picked herself up as she found her sea legs. It was the first dead body that Eden had seen. Eden reached out and touched Nancy gently on the cheek.

As she did so she failed to notice the tiny splash of blood that transferred to her palm. Nancy's skin felt so cold, and cumbersome. Touching it reminded her of touching her own face after she had been anaesthetised at the dentist, it felt numb. Eden imagined the expressions and mannerisms that used to occupy the features that were now so still.

Eden began to feel angry at the pointless waste of human life, this was someone's daughter, someone's best friend, someone's girlfriend. She didn't know how she was going to do it, but she owed it to Nancy to try and find out what happened to her. She had barely known Nancy in life, but in her death they seemed to be intertwined. Eden pulled the sheet over Nancy's face. She couldn't shake the feeling that this whole nightmare was linked to her in some way, but she had no idea how. *Had Nancy been killed because of Eden? Could this whole thing be linked to that night five years ago and what Eden did?*

Eden began to make her way to the exit, until something shiny caught her eye. She walked slowly to the object, but then stopped dead in her tracks. There, taped to the morgue wall, was a Polaroid photograph of Eden that had been taken just minutes before. The image showed Eden standing over Nancy's body, as she touched her cheek. Underneath the image, the words 'LEAVE CANTILLON BEFORE SOMEONE ELSE DIES' were written in deep red.

A stab of panic shot through Eden's body. She span

91

around. The photographer must be in there with her. She snatched the photograph from the wall and ran out the morgue as fast as her shaky legs would carry her. As she clambered up the stairs, her head spinning, she noticed a speck of Nancy's blood on her palm. Eden pulled at her nightgown and rubbed frantically until the stain was removed. The blood was no longer visible, but Eden feared she still had it all over her hands.

Chapter Twelve

Eden dispatched her tray of scrambled eggs on the bedside table and peered through the rain splashed window. The hospital staff were completely bewildered about Eden's misadventure in the early hours of that morning. All staff working the night shift had been formally questioned about the breach in security, and the police had been informed. Eden had, of course, omitted to disclose the small detail of the photograph, but she felt that the authorities had their turn at solving the case, and now it was time to start taking matters into her own hands. It was her life, after all. Whoever did this was not going to scare her away from her home, especially after she had fought so hard to get back to Cantillon. Now all she wanted to do was to get out of the clammy hospital bed and find out who was behind this.

Dr Lister appeared in the doorway, his face stern and unyielding. Eden had hoped that Lister might be sympathetic to her plight, and would allow her to be discharged. But upon seeing him this morning, Eden felt discouraged.

"We do apologise for the unpleasant incident that took place in the morgue earlier this morning. Rest assured hospital staff are adjusting security accordingly." His eyes didn't move from her chart, and Lister's face certainly didn't convey any such acknowledgment. Lister's tone was so matter-of-fact, Eden wondered if she should apologise to him.

"Now then, to the more pressing issue of your health. Quite frankly you seem to be a bit of a medical enigma. The latest batch of blood and urine results reveal that you are back to a normal state of health. In fact, I am pleased to say that you are actually extremely well."

Eden felt the smile begin to take over her mouth, she tried to keep it at bay until he had finished delivering his verdict.

"However, test results taken at the time of admission indicate quite a different story. Follow-up tests suggest that you may have a mild form of a condition called Hyponatremia. In layman's terms it means that you have a slightly lower level of sodium in your blood. The condition is sometimes called Water Intoxication because people that suffer from it may have high levels of water in the body. In more extreme cases water can be absorbed into your body's cells causing headaches, aches and pains, confusion, fainting, hallucinations."

Eden head span as she tried to take in the information.

"Normally we would admit you for a few days, but since your latest results demonstrate that you are back to a normal bill of health, I am minded to keep you in for observation for the next twenty-four hours and discharge you first thing in the morning, assuming your latest results continue to reflect such good news. However, this is on the proviso that there is someone at home to keep a check on you, and should you feel any discomfort, even if it's extremely mild, you must return immediately."

"I will make sure of it, Doctor,' chimed a high-pitched West Cork accent from the doorway. Niamh, Amira, and Riley filled the entrance. Their arms were spilling over with flowers, grapes, chocolates, and more magazines.

"I can see that you will be well taken care of," Lister's face softened for the first time, and with that he disappeared out the door.

"So what is this I hear about a certain person developing quite the fetish for necromancy?"

"Necro what now?" Amira rolled her eyes at Riley.

"You know, hanging out with dead people," Niamh whispered into Amira's ear.

"Eeeew." Amira winced.

"Now, Eden, if you are lonely and in need of some

company, we are here for you. You don't need to cosy up to the body bags in the morgue." Riley's cheeky smile beamed from ear to ear.

"I can always rely on you to lower the bar, Riley." Eden grinned at him. "Some people might consider that a tad insensitive, but thankfully not me. I find your sledgehammer, bordering on a car wreck of a sense of humour, refreshing. In small doses of course."

The arrival of her three friends offered Eden some comfort after a harrowing few hours. She was surprised about just how happy she was to see them. "Anyway don't worry about all that. I am fine now."

"We certainly will worry! You are telling us that, firstly, someone lays in wait in the Banshee's Burrow and try's to do God knows what to you in the dark. And then, the same person goes on to stalk and most probably kill a girl from our year in college. And then, to top matters off, somebody stealthily abducts you in the night and leaves you lying in a morgue, next to that very same girl's dead body, and you don't think we should be worried? Jesus, Eden, are you nuts? You need to take these things seriously. I think you could be in very real danger here." Niamh was speaking at a pitch only dogs could hear.

"I agree with the high pitched one. Eden, you are far from fine." Riley's voice was authoritative and self-assured. "You are a mess. Your health is failing, quite frankly you look like crap. I haven't seen you eat since I met you, and you are clearly on Freddy Krueger's bucket list".

"Jees hold your horses a minute, both of you." Eden retaliated. "First of all, excuse me Riley, but Dr Lister just gave me a clean bill of health, and I may look like crap, but this is how I usually look without make-up! And secondly, Niamh, all I said was that I was fine now. I am totally with you. I have had as much as I can take from this psycho and now I intend to get some answers." Eden's eyes narrowed. "But guys there is more you don't know. I haven't mentioned this to anyone else, but look."

Eden slid her hand under her pillow and produced the

photograph that she found in the morgue.

Three stunned faces looked back at Eden.

"This is getting seriously scary." Amira bit on her lip.

"No offence, Eden, but what the hell did you do? Someone is out to get you and people don't usually unleash the crazy for no reason?" Riley knew immediately that he had gone too far.

"Thanks a lot Riley. I should have guessed that it would wind up being my fault. For your information I have no idea why someone wants me to get a one-way ticket back to Worcestershire." Eden shut her eyes tight and squeezed back tears.

Riley walked meekly over to Eden's bedside and perched on the edge of the mattress. He pulled her head into his shoulder. "Sorry I'm an idiot," he said as he kissed the top of her hair.

"It seems to me that we have two choices." Amira cleared her throat. "We can spend this time arguing, and panicking about Eden. Or we can put our heads together and try and get to the bottom of this. The police are doing their investigation, so why don't we do a little sleuthing of our own?"

"That's the first sensible thing that has been said all morning." Eden smiled.

"Right so what are the facts?" Riley took charge once again. He picked up Eden's hospital chart and turned the top page over to reveal a blank page. He threw the chart, and a pen over to Amira and gestured for her to write notes. She sighed and resumed her usual position of subservience.

"Okay, so we can assume that based on the surveillance footage of the Living Dead Ball, both Nancy and Eden were attacked by the same person." Niamh noted. "We can also conclude that the person in question wore some form of disguise. But can we assume that it was that same person who managed to get into the hospital ward and gain entry to the morgue? Or are we looking at a second person?" Niamh asked.

"Hmm, I don't think it's safe to assume anything at this

stage. It could have been anyone in the hospital," Eden replied.

"Okay, so what questions can we ask?" Riley quizzed in an attempt to move the conversation on to more fruitful avenues of investigation.

"Why kill Nancy? How did they kill Nancy? What do they want with Eden?" Niamh surmised.

"All good questions Niamh, but more importantly why not kill Eden? Why take her to the morgue?"

"They must want her alive for some reason," Amira interjected. "They've had two opportunities to off her and no one has?"

"Can we employ a shred of sensitivity, seen as I am sat right here please?" Eden scowled at the carefree way they were discussing her potential murder.

"Okay so we are getting somewhere." Riley ignored Eden's plea entirely. "From the photograph, we now know for sure that Eden is key to this whole situation, we are just not sure how or why."

"So we know a lot then," Eden said sarcastically as Riley continued.

"Amira – look into the tape again. Use your special 'friend' at the security desk to watch the footage and see if we have missed anything. Niamh – go back to the Banshee's Burrow in the daylight and see if you can find anything that the killer left in there."

"And *you* will…?" Amira and Niamh said in unison.

"I will support Eden at this hard time, and stay at her bedside. Her parents are out the country after all." He propped his feet up on her bed, closed his eyes, and put his hands behind his head.

Eden kicked his legs off, which sent him hurtling off balance onto the floor. "Thank you, Riley. That's ever so thoughtful of you. But I think I would rather Niamh stay with me if it's all the same to you." Eden looked at Niamh. "We can have some girly time, and she makes much better tea than you do."

Niamh smiled and sat in the chair next to Eden.

"Fine, fine. I will check out the stupid Banshee's Burrow then, but if the Banshee eats me then I am blaming you."

"I don't think Banshees eat people, Riley," Eden said trying not to laugh.

"At least we can write this up for Media as our news story I suppose." Riley feigned being heartbroken. He walked over to Eden's bed, kissed her hand and stomped out the hospital room, with Amira in tow.

"See you back in Crookhaven Halls tomorrow?" Eden called after them.

Riley grunted in agreement.

"I think our Riley is a little better at delegating than he is at actually doing." Niamh smiled. "So what do you fancy getting up to then? Shoot some pool, an afternoon swim perhaps? Bowling?"

"All good options Niamh, but I reckon I will just sit here, eat grapes and talk rubbish to you for a few hours."

"Sounds lovely. So let's cut straight to the good stuff. Dylan Blake - how goes it?"

Eden blushed. "You are supposed to build up to that topic, but seen as you brought it up, the whole thing is a total mess. We have been getting on really well and I have loved spending time with him over the last few days. God if I am honest, he's the reason I came back, but..."

"But..."

"But friendship is all that's on the table."

"Is it because of that blonde he's meeting today? Oregan, or something?"

Eden's face went hot. She had forgotten about Oregan amidst all the chaos. The familiar wave of jealousy pulsed through her. Eden did her best to conceal it from Niamh.

"It's just not the right time for Dylan and me. So, erm, what are they supposed to be doing today?"

"Scotty mentioned it yesterday. She's in their Film class and asked Dylan to go to some horror film. I wouldn't worry she's totally weird. Yes, alright, I suppose on the one hand you could say she was attractive." Niamh noticed

Eden's fingers tighten around her mug of tea, and quickly backtracked. "I mean, she's not that attractive. Did I mention that she's totally weird? Shall I say weird again if it makes you feel happier?"

Eden told her mouth to smile at her friend who was so desperately trying to make her feel better. It didn't obey.

"It's fine, Niamh, don't worry. I would much rather know and I am really glad it was you that told me. For the record, though, the weird thing works *for* Oregan, not against her. Dylan likes anything that isn't the norm. He might come across as a typical bloke who loves sport, but there is much more to him than that. He loves the weird and the wonderful."

"Right, well, let's just move on. Later I'll get to the bottom of why you are only extending the hand of friendship to him, but for now it's time to cheer up. So I'm thinking I will get the chocolate, you ask the nurse for another pot of tea, and we can watch some girly films on my laptop. Yes?"

Eden laughed. "Yes. But nothing about romance, strictly comedies only."

"Deal."

The Pearl River Café was crammed with customers. Saturday afternoon in Skull was always busy, even outside tourist season. Zian Tang's little authentic café that specialised in Chinese cuisine was thriving. Amongst the saturated market of Skull fish and chip shops, and more traditional British eateries, it was a bohemian and exotic environment, and both qualities were uncommon on the mainland.

The table nearest the door was occupied by a ladies coffee morning. Five middle-aged women squawked and howled at each other's jokes as they tucked into their noodles and soups. Next to them sat a teenage couple on their first date having awkward conversations above the noise. Zian brought out a tray of orders and impressively snaked around the tables, delivering the tray to the cushioned area at the back of the restaurant. The words 'River Garden' were stencilled on the wall.

The River Garden section was filled with low tables and customers sitting cross-legged on the floor. Oregan and Dylan were deep in conversation. They didn't even notice the food arrive. Oregan's long blonde hair was wild around one shoulder. She wore flowers interspersed in her thick locks, her long black lace dress was arranged in a perfect circle on the floor, covering her legs entirely. She had ordered the jellyfish and cucumber salad, she used chopsticks as confidently as the Chinese.

Dylan, unlike Oregan, was struggling with the whole situation. As he had grown from boy to man, strength and muscles had come at the expense of flexibility. He could hardly bend his legs, and certainly couldn't sit cross-legged. He had also never used chopsticks and scarcely ate adventurous food. Usually he loved to try new things, but food was where he drew the line. Dylan thought about roast dinners as he stared at his cold jellyfish salad and wished he hadn't muttered the words 'make that two,' as Oregan ordered using the Chinese translation. When Zian delivered the food and set it down in front of him he immediately realised the magnitude of his error. He was reminded of the chilled monkey brains in *Indiana Jones and The Temple of Doom* as he attempted to pick up the slimy wet pieces of what he thought was quite frankly crunchy plastic. He dribbled the sesame oil down his chin, then decided that eating was overrated and picked up his Chinese tea.

After analysing the film and concluding that *Videodrome,* much like Hideo Nakata's *Ringu,* is one of those rare films that is actually more impacting when seen on the small screen, due to the fact that the narrative centres around a videotape, Oregan moved the conversation on to more personal matters.

"So are you seeing anyone at the moment?" Oregan's directness took Dylan by surprise for the second time since they met, he was much more of a 'round the houses' kind of person. He looked at her for a few moments before he answered, Eden's words from yesterday still ringing in his ears.

"No, not really. Yes, I would say no." They both laughed at his ridiculous answer; the tension between them faded.

"You don't sound sure about that." Oregan's big eyes narrowed as they fixed on Dylan, she skilfully picked up another piece of jellyfish without looking at her plate. Dylan wondered how she could be so intense, but simultaneously appear laid back and relaxed. He couldn't recall another seventeen year old who was so self-assured and comfortable in their own skin.

"Dylan, you don't have to be afraid of what you say to me. I will be frank, as I have never had much time for games. I like you. I think we have similar interests. I don't know anyone else who will talk horror with me and watch extreme movies, and not think I am a complete psychopath, or at the very least a bit weird."

"You are a bit weird." Dylan's smile was big and bold.

Oregan's laughter interrupted her own monologue. She continued, "You are too! How many Skulldonian FC players watch horror movies with strange little Goth girls they hardly know, and eat Chinese food with their hands?"

"I said you were weird not strange, and can we just skip straight past the eating thing. It's been mortifying enough." They laughed, Dylan began to feel relaxed around her, and for a few moments he genuinely didn't think about Eden.

"Should I put your vague answer, to what can only be described as a simple question, down to that pretty brunette I have seen you with? Eden is it?"

The mention of Eden's name made Dylan feel a pang. "You might say that, yes."

"So…" She gestured for him to continue,

"We used to know each other a long time ago, and then she went away, and now…"

"She's back." Oregan's words were loaded and hung in the air.

"I don't know where it's going, or what it even is between us."

"It's completely fine Dylan. Let's change the subject. Tell me about Eden."

"That's not exactly what I would call changing the subject."

Oregan gave him a scornful look that made him start talking instantly.

"Well, she's not unlike yourself, actually. Drawn to the dark side, not dark fiction particularly, but more a dark sense of humour, and she has always been rebellious. As a kid she was literally the most lively, strong, and exciting person, just to be around her was an adventure. And now she still has that kind of magnetism that draws you in, but..." Dylan hesitated as he caught himself and realised how confessional he had become, "but she has now lost her light, her sparkle I suppose, she seems..."

"Damaged?" Oregan found the word for him.

Dylan stared at Oregan. Her observation had been uncannily close to the truth. Something about her intuition in that moment made him feel uneasy. The waitress arrived at their table to clear the plates. Dylan passed over his jellyfish salad bowl, a strategically placed napkin disguised a multitude of sins.

Dylan and Oregan left the café and spilled out into the night sky.

"Can I walk you home? After what happened to that poor John Fisher girl it might not be safe to be out after dark."

"That's very sweet Dylan, but don't worry about me I assure you I can take care of myself."

Dylan smiled, he didn't doubt it.

"I don't live far and I'm going to pick up a few things from a friend's house en route. They only live down there." She gestured behind her to a small plot of houses that sat on a hill.

"If you are sure then. Thanks for today it's been ..." Dylan deliberately trailed off and grinned at her.

"Hasn't it?" Oregan smiled, kissed him on the cheek and walked away. Dylan stood there for a few moments and sighed as he watched her leave. When he woke up this morning he planned to cancel their meeting, but quickly realised that he didn't have Oregan's phone number. His upbringing prevented him from even considering the prospect of standing her up, so he settled on attending the screening and was going to leave straight after the credits. Dylan didn't think he would enjoy himself as much as he did. This was an unexpected complication.

Heavy in thought, Dylan turned and began the long walk home. A storm was brewing, the rain began to fall from the black sky, the wind howled and made the dry leaves dance on the roadside. Dylan turned up his collar and walked briskly; he didn't notice the footsteps that followed his own.

A few moments later Dylan stood at the gate to Holly Cottage. He wondered how he had got there. Dylan wanted to know more about Eden, and couldn't wait for his mum to decide whether she was going to let him in on the family secret. He was left with no other option. He hadn't spoken to Eden since she telephoned her parents, they could be on their way back to Skull at that very moment. Upon their return they would certainly clean the house and dispense with its contents, so it was now or never. He opened the creaky gate and made his way to the front door. He hadn't thought about how he was going to break into the house. If Eden were with him, she could have slid her tiny arm through the letterbox, but there was no way that Dylan was going to even get his wrist through. As the overgrown bushes parted and the door came into view, he realised that entry was no longer an issue.

Someone had beaten Dylan to it. The door was open and the place had been ransacked. Every inch of floor was covered with the Hollow's personal items; picture frames, notebooks, and shattered china ornaments were strewn everywhere. But what would someone want with the cottage after all these years? Dylan began to feel genuinely worried for Eden, it seemed increasingly likely that someone seriously wanted to hurt her.

Dylan took a deep breath and walked into the dark. The cottage lights were disconnected years ago. He fumbled around in his jean pockets and pulled out a football-shaped torch that Beth had brought him a few years ago. He carefully negotiated his way around the entrance hall and into the library to see if the intruder had discovered Charles's secret hidey-hole. Thankfully it was just as he left it. Given the circumstances, Dylan decided it was sensible to transport the entire contents into his bag. Charles' most private possessions would be safer with him, and this way he could look into the evidence and make an informed decision about Eden. He scooped up the numerous envelopes, some accounts books, and a rather scary looking metal and pearl antique, and placed them carefully in his Adidas rucksack.

Dylan walked quickly to the front door. He turned off the torch and slipped the rucksack over his shoulder so he could unlock the latch and let himself out. As the torchlight went out and he plummeted into darkness, he felt a chill pass over him. *Hadn't he left the front door open?* Glancing around Dylan opened the front door and exited the cottage. He quickly picked up pace, and in a slow jog put some distance between himself and Holly Cottage. He really hated that old place.

Dylan was taken aback to see his dad's Silver BMW parked in the driveway. "Brilliant," he muttered under his breath. The last time his mother had allowed his father to come over, was when Dylan and Scotty got suspended from school for repeatedly saying the word spoon to their teacher, Mr Spoonhead. Dylan wondered what this could possibly be about. He put the key into the lock and took his second deep breath of the evening as he walked into the living room.

Kieran Blake sat awkwardly in the familiar brown leather chair that he used to sit in night after night. Judy was wearing a hole in the carpet with her frantic pacing.

"Where on earth have you been?" Judy looked enraged,

but she was suddenly hugging him as if her life depended on it.

Dylan shooed her away. "Mum, I am seventeen. I am old enough to move out, get married, drive a car, have a child myself for Christ sake. I don't need to explain myself to you all the time."

"Don't speak to your mother like that."

Dylan knew his father was just attempting to score some much needed brownie points from his mother, so decided not to retaliate. He would much rather they got on, even if it was at his expense.

"I'm sorry Mum, I didn't mean to be short with you, I have just had a day of it. Look, can we just skip straight to the reason we are having this little Blake reunion?"

At that moment Beth walked in, a sandwich in her mouth. She looked up at their grave faces and stepped straight back out without saying a word. Dylan went to call after her, thinking there would be safety in numbers, but decided to spare her the awkwardness. He heard her feet stomp up the stairs and wished he could follow them.

"Fine, you want to be treated like an adult, then that's what we will do. But you have to be ready to deal with the consequences. The decisions we have to make aren't easy, son, and sometimes you have to do the hardest thing, even if it makes your life difficult in the short term."

"Okay, this sounds heavy Dad. I think I will sit down."

Kieran decanted two glasses of Jameson's whiskey and passed his son the crystal tumbler. Dylan sipped the drink, ignoring the taste as best he could. For Dylan, the moment was about a rite of passage, not the actual act of drinking alcohol. He still didn't have the taste for it, he wondered when he would suddenly enjoy, rather than endure a drink.

"Eden's parents are not Charles and Delia."

Dylan choked on his whiskey. He was not expecting the revelation. "Go on". He tried to sound calm, and didn't want to spook his father from divulging the full story.

Judy finally stopped pacing and sat down on the leather chesterfield. She was calmer now the dirty little secret had been announced.

"We don't know the whole truth. We have put together bits and pieces over the years. It started seventeen years ago. Your mother had an antenatal group when she got pregnant with you. Needless to say, Delia was not a member. But we knew the Hollows pretty well back then, we used to socialise quite a bit, mainly because your mother and Delia got on so well. Delia was a kind person, she was really rather lovely, but Charles was a bit stiff. Anyway, a year or so after your mother had you, the Hollows went on holiday. The whole thing was very strange. They left suddenly in the small hours without telling a soul. They didn't lock up. They didn't put the bins out. Their front gate was swinging in the wind the whole time they were away. I suppose it's funny the details you remember so many years later, but in those days people didn't just up and leave. They planned holidays all year and spoke to their neighbours so that they could watch the house. Not like today at all."

"Dad, could we stay on track?" Dylan found his dad's digression annoying on a normal day, but during this conversation it was infuriating.

"Sorry, so they returned after six weeks, and they had with them a tiny new born baby. They came up with some cock and bull story about Delia not knowing she was pregnant, and her having underlying health issues. Most people believed it, and perhaps we would have, if it wasn't for your mother and Delia's friendship. One night, just before their supposed holiday, Delia and your mother stayed up drinking a bottle of wine whilst Charles and I were at a golf tournament. Delia confided in your mother that her marriage was a sham. She said that she and Charles were only married in name and had not shared a bed in over three years. To top things off, she told your mother that the real trouble began when they discovered it was impossible for them to have children. Three months later Eden arrived, by immaculate conception it would seem. After that, Delia and your mother never regained their closeness. Delia could hardly face us."

106

Dylan sat back and digested the information. It was a great deal to take in.

"So, who are Eden's parents?"

"We don't know, darling." Judy dabbed the tears that escaped from her eyes. "But this isn't our business, Dylan. It's not our place. It must stay between us. Every family has their tragedies."

Dylan looked at his mother and how upset she had become. He couldn't bear to see her that way, but he had to stand up for what he believed in. This was untrodden ground for him, for all of them. He momentarily missed the clarity of childhood.

"I am so sorry, Mum, but I can't promise that. As you said, Dad, these decisions are difficult and if the last few years of growing up have taught me anything, it's that the world is grey, not black and white. You are just going to have to trust me and my judgement. I promise that whatever I decide to do will be with Eden's best interests at heart, but that's the only promise I can make, I'm afraid."

And with that, the conversation was over and the brown leather chair was empty once again.

Chapter Thirteen

The undergrowth was thick. Drips of rain water slopped from the leaves. *It* sat there waiting, watching him. The foggy, grey weather reduced visibility. *It* could barely see past a few metres. His tall, broad frame manoeuvred with unexpected agility as he climbed the rocks to get to the beach. He was looking for something, following a path.

It approached the rocks, keeping low to ensure the element of surprise. *It* watched his flesh move around under his clothes. He was lean but there was certainly a lot to go around. A perfect selection, *It* thought. Now was the time to move. The waves crashed loudly and the spray caused an even thicker mist. He didn't see the shadows as they enveloped him. He didn't smell the stench, but he did hear a sound he had never heard before. At first it was more of a vibration that grew deafening. He was debilitated, clutching his ears in both hands to try and stop them from hearing it, his head felt so much pressure, he thought it may explode. He dropped to his knees, and then there was nothing.

His eyelids flickered open and shut. Muffled noises became clearer, nearer. His body felt wet, soaking. He was in pain, the freezing bite of the water stabbed at his flesh like tiny needles. His eyes were open now, the horror of his circumstance dawned on him. He couldn't breathe, there was water in his lungs. He was in the middle of the ocean, stranded in the pitch black. He frantically felt his skin. What was he wearing, a wetsuit? Something had kept him from dying of hypothermia, but he knew he didn't have long. Something slimy clung to his hands as he moved them around in the water. He quickly splashed it away, whatever it was smelt awful. He stopped treading water for a second as he realised he could float. He was supported by something. He felt weightless. His legs and arms went still, but he didn't sink. His body just bobbed from side to side. A float suit perhaps, an inbuilt life jacket? The top of the suit did feel padded. Hundreds of questions flashed through his mind. There was nothing around him just miles and miles of sea. The pain in his legs grew stronger, it was throbbing. This couldn't just be from the cold. He was so confused. He span around and stuck his head under the water, but couldn't see anything apart from the strange gloopy substance under the black murky water. He traced his fingers down his left thigh, to his knee and then bent his leg to feel his foot. He started the awkward process again with the right leg, down his thigh, to his knee, but there was no longer a lower leg to bend. The pain became agony as his brain now acknowledged the injury. He cried aloud, the water looked black as it was interspersed with his blood. Terror set in as the next thing he heard was a swishing noise behind him. He didn't need to turn around to see the dorsal fin as it rose out the water.

Chapter Fourteen

Sunday afternoon was dark and rainy. Dr Lister signed Eden's discharge papers that morning and arranged for her to be transported back to her halls of residence. There would be some exploratory tests as an out-patient in the near future, but for now, Eden had the all clear. She put the key in the lock and opened the door. She closed her eyes and breathed in the familiar smell of her dormitory. The blend of salty sea air, fused with sweet perfume and lavender bed sheets, was the new scent of her home, and she loved it. Her room was so warm. After two nights in the hospital it felt like stepping into a hot bath, as she kicked off her pumps. Even the carpet felt softer than she had remembered.

Eden walked over to the balcony to check her weather station. It had been several days since she had taken her last reading. As she crossed the dormitory floor, Eden stopped in her tracks, noticing the new additions to her bedroom. Every window ledge, sideboard and table, brimmed with beautiful porcelain flower pots, each of them housing a different type of daisy. *Dylan*, she thought as her whole face smiled. She examined each pot and took out a small card bearing an image of two children playing happily in the garden. The little girl held a worm in her hands and dangled it menacingly in the little boy's direction. The little boy was covered in dirt and smiled at his friend as he offered her a solitary daisy. Eden turned the card over. Dylan had inscribed a quotation, she still recognised his messy scrawl.

Eden

Daisies (also known as the Thunderflower) may appear to be one complete flower, but they actually comprise of two different types of flower: disk florets and white ray florets. The disk florets exist as the centre of the flower, whilst the white florets exist on the periphery.

So, whilst daisies may give the overall impression of being one complete whole, they actually consist of two parts, and when separated neither part can, or indeed should, function without the other.

I am glad you are home.
Dylan

Eden wiped a tear from her eye. She carefully placed the card in a small shoe box that she kept under her bed. She wished Dylan could be there now so she could tell him everything, but she would have to wait until later that afternoon and try and steal a few moments alone with him. Word had already spread that she was back at Crookhaven, and the group had decided to meet up and discuss updates on the case.

Niamh was on her way back from her sailing club and, unsurprisingly, due to her love of food, had opted to fulfil the food order. Dylan and Scotty had managed to get some alcohol using Scotty's brother ID card. Amira and Riley would also be along shortly. In just a few days she had more family in Skull than she had ever had in Worcestershire.

A loud vibrating noise yanked Eden from her thoughts, a photo of Amira wearing a trilby hat flashed up on Eden's phone. Eden switched the phone to loud speaker as she walked towards her closet and pulled out her dressing gown.

"Hi Eden, how you feeling? You missing the smell of Milton and the food that tastes like vomit?"

Eden pulled her T-shirt over her head and kicked off her jeans.

"I have settled back in just fine, thank you. I even

111

missed the spider above my bed that is intent on killing the insect population of Cantillon and offering them to me as a sacrifice." Eden put on her dressing gown and stood on her bed to inspect the recent casualties.

"How delightful. Anyway, I won't be long as I'm seeing you in a couple of hours. But I am just at the library and thought I would fill you in on my sleuthing."

"Great. Probably best to do it now before the others arrive." Eden brushed her teeth and began to run a bath.

"So, first off, I have drawn a blank with the surveillance footage. The files have been embargoed by Skull Police, so no more screenings I'm afraid."

"Damn. I guess we should have expected that," Eden shouted from the bathroom.

"Hopefully Riley will have found something a little more useful at the Banshee's Burrow. I did find out some info that does shed a bit of light on Nancy's murder though."

Eden threw down her toothbrush, ran into her bedroom and snatched up the phone.

"I'm listening."

"So I was checking out back issues of *The Skull Herald* for our Citizen Journalism Media assignment, and I began to notice that Nancy certainly isn't the first strange disappearance in Cantillon. I ended up checking the missing persons sections of the last two years of newspapers, and it turns out that there are five missing persons that are still unaccounted for. All of them went missing from Cantillon or off the coast of Skull. All of the disappearances are people under the age of twenty, so they are often blamed on drink and drugs or holidaymakers getting lost, that type of thing. They are all similar in age, oddly enough they are all similar looking, not hair colour or anything, but they are all physically fit people, sporty types. Hang on, I have the list here."

Eden couldn't believe what she was hearing. She waited for Amira to come back to the phone.

"Okay, so a female lifeguard aged nineteen goes missing off the coast of Skull in January last year. A twenty year old man goes missing just two miles away in the July. A fifteen year old local girl from Skull also goes missing in December last year. And a couple aged seventeen go missing in June of this year after taking the Cantillon-Skull Ferry."

"So if you include Nancy, that is six," Eden said in disbelief.

"And counting, I am afraid."

"I can't believe that no-one has put this together."

"I know. This is seriously dark stuff. They didn't exactly put 'a severely limited life expectancy' under the employability section of the college prospectus did they? Anyway, I have to run. I am getting dirty looks from the college librarian for being on my phone. I will see you soon and we can explain it to Riley and the others."

With that, the phone went dead.

Eden sat on the edge of her bed for a moment, feeling shell shocked. She stared into space and tried to decide what she was going to do with the newfound information. Her thoughts were interrupted as she noticed that her phone was flashing. She had an unread message. Eden absentmindedly opened it.

At first Eden couldn't quite make out what she was looking at. She zoomed in a little and lightened the image.

There in the middle of a frame was what appeared to be a stuffed deer's head hanging on the wall. As she magnified the image further, Eden saw that one of the antlers was drenched in blood and there were a few strands of hair hanging from it. In the background of the photograph she saw the glass cabinet containing the familiar manikin that she recognised from the night of the attack. This was the Banshee's Burrow. She scrolled down to read the message.

Looks like you injured it. See you soon. R.

Riley's message was brief, but to the point. Eden was suddenly angry with herself - how could she have forgotten such an important detail? The night of the attack she had pushed her assailant away as hard as she could and heard them scream out in pain. Whoever had attacked her was injured and, therefore, whoever attacked her was *identifiable*.

Eden wished that Niamh was at home. She hated not being able to discuss such colossal news with someone. She would have to try and block out the conversation with Amira, and Riley's message, until the others arrived. There was nothing she could do in the immediate future, so she would just have to focus on the job at hand, and the practicalities of getting the venue ready for her guests. As she bent down to pick up the jeans and T-shirt that she had flung on the floor moments earlier, she caught a glimpse of her reflection in the balcony window. Riley was right, she had some serious work to do. She had lost weight, her skin was pale, and her eyes had retreated into her face. She was beginning to look seriously ill. Eden opened the bathroom cabinet and picked up a bottle of instant fake tan. Her mother always said that a bit of colour made everyone look less dead. It was quite amazing what a bottle of fake-bake, and a generous application of makeup could do. Eden sunk into her bath and tried not to think about Nancy.

Eden checked her watch, they should have been here ten minutes ago. There was no sign of anyone. After two days of isolation and lying in bed all day, she couldn't sit on her own a minute longer. She grabbed some overdue library books and pulled on Niamh's black raincoat, her own coat was creased and still damp from the storm chase. Last of all she squished her feet awkwardly into her floral Wellington Boots and bounded out the door. She pulled up her hood and began to make her way to the college's main building. The rain was heavier than it looked from her balcony window, it splashed at her face. Perhaps a walk was not the best course of action after all. Eden had just straightened her hair, and couldn't bear the thought of having to repeat the mundane process. The library books could certainly wait.

Eden began to turn around and make her way back to her dorm, but out of the corner of her eye she caught a glimpse of something. At first she didn't know why she had stopped to take a better look at the couple, and then she realised that there was something familiar about them. They were standing very close, sharing an umbrella. The girl was smiling and laughing and looked as though she was thoroughly enjoying the company of her partner. She couldn't see the boy's face, but she didn't need to - it was Dylan and Oregan. Eden felt the deep pang of disappointment, but she couldn't bring herself to look away. There seemed to be an intimacy between them. She feared that Oregan was no longer 'just another girl from Dylan's Film class'.

The girl's wet face glanced over in Eden's direction. There was a glimmer of recognition as she gestured to Dylan to turn around. Upon seeing Eden, Dylan realigned his posture and doubled the space between him and Oregan. His body adjusted and became full of self-awareness, every movement contrived and unnatural. The pair walked over and Eden braced herself for the awkward moment. She knew she had to speak first. She wanted to appear casual and unaffected by their chance meeting, when actually every cell in her body was turning green with jealousy.

"Hi Dylan. Thanks for the flowers, that was so sweet. Hi err… Oregan is it?"

Once again Oregan simply shot Eden a half smile and looked back at Dylan. She clearly didn't want to engage with Eden in any way.

"Eden, it's so good to see you back on your feet. I was just making my way over to yours from the library when I bumped into Oregan."

It was so cold. Eden could see Dylan's breath, yet his cheeks looked as if they were on fire.

"I am just heading back to my place now actually. I will see you a bit later then?"

After Oregan's refusal to engage, Eden just wanted to run away and put an end to this horrendous moment.

"Great. I will come with you." Dylan moved from Oregan's side to Eden's in one quick step. Dylan and Eden both waited for Oregan to make her excuses and be on her way, but instead she just stood there, and lingered in the moment. It was as though she revelled in the awkwardness.

Eden couldn't bare the silence any more. "Oregan, you are welcome to join us. We are having a bit of a party round mine." Eden couldn't bring herself to be cruel to anyone, but at that moment she hated herself for such admirable qualities.

"Okay, sounds good." Oregan resumed her place at the other side of Dylan. The unusual threesome walked in silence back to Crookhaven.

Once inside, Eden provided Oregan with a seat and began to busy herself with making them both a cold drink. Dylan looked from Oregan to Eden. Both women were beautiful in different ways. If he had met either woman without the other his life would most certainly be less complicated. Oregan was mysterious. She was so wonderfully different. There was something almost ethereal about her that left him wanting to know more. He wanted to learn about her, to see where she lived, what her room looked like, what her family were like. But then there was Eden. She was equally striking, with her dark hair, and olive complexion. She was an Amazonian beauty masquerading in jeans and a T-shirt. But she was also so much more than looks. He couldn't articulate the way he felt about her. In a way it was automatic, without question. Perhaps it was instinctive. Rationalising his feeling for her was like trying to explain how to laugh or cry, it was ingrained in him. He didn't know if that was necessarily a healthy way to feel, but all he knew was that when she hurt, he hurt. Like some tragic empath, he was entwined in her world.

A knock on the door yanked Dylan from his daydream. Scotty walked in and put down a crate of beer. He eyed the odd threesome and grinned from ear to ear. Of course he couldn't refrain from commenting on the situation.

"Hi guys. Hot in here, isn't it? Dylan, you look a bit flushed. You all right? Bet you could do with a beer.' He threw Dylan a bottle of San Miguel, Scotty's grin stretched wider and wider. "Let's have a little music, shall we?"

Dylan watched Scotty's face grow in excitement as he scrolled through Eden's back catalogue searching for the perfect song. Dylan flinched as he knew what was coming. The sound of Britney Spears' 'Womaniser' pumped through the dormitory. Dylan jumped to his feet and silently kicked Scotty who was dancing to the music, and quickly switched the song to something more innocuous. At that moment Niamh arrived home. As she opened the door her face was completely hidden behind the pile of pizza boxes that she was carrying. As Niamh carefully delivered them to the work surface she eyed Oregan, her face became thunderous. As Dylan introduced Niamh and Oregan, Niamh's usual celtic warmth was replaced by an icy exterior that was obvious for all to see. She looked at Eden across the room and mouthed the words, "What the hell?"

Niamh went into the small kitchen area and began to serve the takeaway. Eden followed in her wake. "We'll talk later. I had to invite her," Eden whispered.

"You, my girl, are too nice," Niamh said a little too loudly. "What time are Riley and Amira arriving?"

There was a loud bang at the dormitory door.

"Speak of the devil," Eden said, turning the door handle.

Eden's smile quickly faded to a frown. Amira's face was grey. She was out of breath, a solitary tear escaped from the corner of her red-raw eyes. Scotty instinctively put his arms around her and supported her as she walked in the door. She tried to speak, but the words didn't come. Eden stared at her and looked over at Niamh. The girls simultaneously realised the source of her upset and desperately hoped they were wrong. One word left both their lips.

"Riley."

THE SERPENT

Chapter Fifteen

The ocean salivated. The tiny Cabin Cruiser bounced up and down precariously, the water frothed and splattered as it met the rain. The black waves swelled as the ocean sucked the boat in and spat it out, like a rippling monster. A world of wonder bubbled below, the creatures of the deep skulked under the surface.

It was dark and the pale faced crew huddled inside the cabin. Dylan, Scotty, and Oregan sat around a small table whilst Amira leaned against the cabin window; her red eyes looked over the ocean. Nobody spoke, they watched the bleak horizon.

Eden accompanied Niamh at the elevated helm station, it was a small space that forced the girls close. They whispered to each other in the moonlight as the rain patted their hoods. Eden looked emaciated and grey. This morning was just like any other Sunday, but the last few hours ensured that today would be forever imprinted on all of their memories, and they feared there was worse to come. For Eden it was a day that would literally shape her character. There was no going back now and, even if she wanted to, there was nowhere for her to go. Her history had been undone.

It had started just after Amira arrived at Eden's dormitory and delivered the news that Riley had not returned home after going to the Banshee's Burrow. The group decided to split up so they could cover as much ground as possible in their search for Riley. In time, the police would conduct their own search, but Riley had not yet been missing for twenty-four hours, a full-scale hunt was not protocol. Matters needed to be taken into hand, especially with the storm brewing. The group knew that they had a short window of opportunity to find him.

Once again, Eden's health was failing. Amira and Niamh suggested that the boys stay in the dormitory with Eden whilst they attend the Carnival. The girls could then circulate pictures of Riley amongst Carnival staff, in the hope that someone remembered him. To both Amira and Niamh's surprise, Oregan elected to join them.

Once the three girls arrived at the Carnival they decided it would be advantageous to separate, so Niamh divided up the three Carnival 'villages' between them. Niamh was charged with working the Freak Show, whilst Amira focused on the Haunted Carousel, and Oregan checked out the Forest of Burlesque. Niamh's section included the beach and the Banshee's Burrow, and whilst her exploration of the Burrow established very little, she did receive a lead from the neighbouring Sword Swallowers, who not only identified Riley from the photograph, but saw him leave the Carnival late last night, after the last ferry crossing. The Sword Swallowers were quite sure that Riley made his way back to the harbour, in order to board his own private vessel.

Whilst Amira found this information rather bewildering, as Riley had never mentioned owning his own boat, it was the only lead they had – they had to follow it. Like many locals, Riley had grown up around boats, so he would certainly be capable of sailing. Riley's family were also incredibly wealthy, so Amira surmised that borrowing his parent's boat would not be completely out of the question. The girls decided that the best course of action was to charter a vessel themselves and go looking for Riley. Niamh's boat Leviathan was moored at Cantillon so, without delay, the girls began to make their way back to Eden's room to fetch the others.

Meanwhile, back at Crookhaven Halls, Eden, Dylan, and Scotty busied themselves searching Riley's room. Riley was also a resident of Crookhaven and occupied the dormitory directly below Eden's. Eden sat cross-legged on the floor and began to empty the contents of Riley's drawer in the hope she would find something, anything, that might lead them to his whereabouts. As she continued to rifle through Riley's private belongings, Eden felt increasingly feverish. Bile began to gather in her mouth, her tummy turned over. She couldn't risk projectile vomiting in front of the boys, so she quickly made her excuses and went back to the solitude of her own room. She vomited violently for what seemed like an eternity. As she watched the water flush around the toilet bowl, her head propped up on her hands, she began to wonder if her illness was some form of retribution. It seemed as though her sickness intensified whenever she was close to Dylan. Perhaps on some buried, subconscious level, her illness was psychosomatic. Could her emotional turmoil have manifested into a physical illness that was literally keeping them apart? Was she doing this to herself?

Eden slid along the floor and collapsed onto her bed. The crack in the top right hand corner of the ceiling was now empty, the spider had found a new home. Eden closed her eyes and drifted in and out of sleep. She dreamt of her father, she could see the name Charles Hollow etched in black script on antique ivory writing paper. As she waned between sleep and lucidity, she began to realise that this was no longer just a dream. At first she couldn't quite make out the words, but then dark black shapes that spelled out her father's name were just about visible in the distance. She tried to focus her eyes. She strained to see. With all her might, Eden extracted herself from her bed and limped over to the letters. Through a haze of nausea, Eden bent down and plucked an envelope from a blue Adidas backpack which sat in the middle of her bedroom floor. She collapsed onto the ground, opened the letter, and began to read.

Dylan walked into Eden's bedroom moments later, but it was too late. The poison had already seeped in. Eden was changed forever, she was heartbroken. Her family's blood didn't run through her veins, worse still, she had no idea who's did. All those years of people telling her that she was so much like her mother, but had her father's green eyes, meant nothing now. She knew nothing about herself. Everything she thought she knew just fell away. That night, five years ago, haunted her every day since, but it now made much more sense. The events of that evening had planted seeds of doubt in her mind, doubt about who and what she was. She had tried to rationalise them and to pretend she imagined the entire episode. After all this time she no longer trusted her own memories. But now she knew – of course she couldn't be their child. How could she be anyone's?

Dylan hadn't spoken since he walked in and bore witness to Eden's heartbreak, as her world literally imploded before his very eyes. He wanted so much to explain why he didn't tell her about her grandmothers letter, why he had caused her to feel so much pain. But he knew that the only function that would serve was to appease his own guilt. Right now, Eden was the only one who mattered, he needed to forget himself. He knelt on the floor in front of her, put her hands in his, and began the story of when he discovered the letter.

***

"Jesus Christ, Eden. I can't believe what I am hearing." Niamh momentarily released Leviathan's wheel and grabbed her friend. She hugged her tightly, the rain from Eden's coat splattered her in the face as she did so. The boat jerked from side to side as the girls embraced. They both had tears in their eyes. "So what on earth are you going to do now? About your parents, sorry not your parents, I mean …" Niamh turned the same colour as her hair as she trampled over the details of Eden's life.

"I know what you mean, Niamh, it's fine. I think you and I are well past the walking-on-eggshells phase. Besides,

124

I rely on you to say it how it is. To be honest, I don't know what I am going to do. Nothing for the moment. I need to find Riley and stop feeling like death before I can sort this mess out. Maybe then I will have it out with them I suppose."

"Will you look for your other parents, I mean the biological ones?"

"I don't know. I guess so. Depending on why they decided not to keep me of course, they might not want to be found." Eden's voice cracked, Niamh extended a hand to Eden and placed it gently on her shoulder. Eden shooed it away and feigned being okay.

"Some things do make more sense now, though. I understand why we never saw my grandmother, and why my own mother never talked about being pregnant, or my birth. I would ask her about it, but she would always avoid the question. In hindsight, she didn't want to lie to me I guess, which is a little redeeming. But then again my whole existence is something of a lie, so I suppose she may as well have made up another fantastic story." Eden was angry, she felt the fury bubbling away inside her. She carefully readjusted herself. She couldn't unlock that door, and let out her rage. She knew it ran deep, and once it escaped she wasn't sure what would be left of her.

"And, of course, it certainly explains why your parents were so adverse to you returning to Skull after all these years. They were probably terrified you would find out their secret."

"My mother's face was so pale when she waved me off. It was as though she were looking at a ghost. I guess in some ways she was. I am the ghost of the child they never had. My presence was with them for a while, but it would never truly stick." Eden trailed off.

Without warning, the boat lunged and made a grinding sound. Metal scraped metal, the girls were thrown off balance. Eden scrambled around on the floor trying to find something to hold on to, but then it just stopped.

Everything went quiet and still.

Dylan flew out of the cabin and climbed the ladder to the upper deck. In seconds he was with her once again. She felt his arms around her as he pulled her to her feet. Scotty helped Amira to hers, as she had been thrown outside the cabin onto the floor.

"Are you alright?" Dylan's face was grave.

"What the hell happened?" They both looked at Niamh for answers.

"I have no idea."

"It felt like we were being pulled downwards?" Eden said with confusion.

"Yeah, it felt as though we were being sucked under." Amira joined the others at the helm.

Scotty's face wore an expression that his friends had not seen before. His wide grin had contorted into a frown, his eyes were closed.

"Scotty, mate. Are you all right?"

"Shhh. Listen." Scotty interrupted Dylan. They both looked out to sea.

"What are we supposed to be hearing?"

"Just listen."

Dylan knew Scotty was not joking around. Scotty was so rarely serious. Dylan hardly recognised his friend.

"Do you hear that?"

The others strained their ears but heard nothing.

"No waves crashing, no rain pelting, no winds howling. Nothing."

They all stood in what appeared to be the eye of a storm. In the distance, surrounding them on all sides, was a ferocious monsoon. Thick black towering clouds were illuminated as lightning lit up the sky and thunder rumbled, but their surroundings were quite tranquil. It was as though the ocean was afraid to move.

"This doesn't make any sense." Eden looked around her, as she tried to read the sky. "This is seriously not right. The storm isn't due for hours yet, and even if it were a storm we can't be in the eye, it defies all science and logic. It just can't be."

"Then how come it is?" Scotty's voice was stern.

"Right, this is too weird. Everyone downstairs into the cabin, now. Niamh, turn the engine off and come with us." Dylan was not going to ask twice.

Once inside, the group huddled together and waited. Minutes passed by but nothing changed. The extreme silence and calm became increasingly menacing.

Eden removed her sodden jacket and walked over to the cabin window, she was burning up from her fever. She watched the waves swelling and thrashing in the distance and couldn't comprehend how the water around them was so comparatively placid. Their part of the ocean was completely still and black, it looked more like oil than water. Dylan stood silently next to her.

"What's that on your back?" Dylan spun Eden around, his voice full of urgency and concern. "Did you cut yourself when you fell?"

"I don't think so."

"There is blood on your back?"

Eden had a patch of dark red blood that had mixed with water on the top of her shoulder blades.

Dylan continued to search for a wound. "That is weird, I can't find a wound? I don't think it's your blood?"

Eden and Dylan looked at each other in confusion.

Eden's head emptied of all thought, as the boat violently jolted and she slammed into the cabin window, the glass shattered on impact.

The floor sank below them and water came flooding in.

There was an overwhelming downward sensation as the boat was sucked below the surface.

Then the boat shot up. Whatever was dragging it down had momentarily let go.

Eden splashed under the water and desperately tried to find her footing, her bloody forehead throbbed with pain.

The cabin lights went out.

There was screaming and widespread panic as the boat lunged downwards once again.

Amira was crying, as the water flooded in and rose to

127

waist level.

Scotty swam over to Amira and lifted her out of the water in one easy motion. She seemed weightless compared to his Viking strength. He placed her safely on the table before climbing up there himself.

Dylan needed to get to Eden, they had become separated in the chaos. He could see her immersed in the water behind some floating furniture, her head oozed with blood. He pulled himself out the water and balanced on a narrow sideboard that stretched around the entire cabin. He carefully made his way over to her and Oregan.

But when he reached them, he saw that Oregan was changed.

Oregan stood in the water. She was completely still and, despite the chaos, appeared to be in total control. She pulled Eden's head above the surface and directed her towards the sideboard.

"G-E-T O-U-T O-F T-H-E W-A-T-E-R." Oregan's words were deep and gravelly.

Dylan stared at Oregan, no longer recognising the speaker. He followed Oregan's gaze and there, weaving in and out of the floating furniture, was an enormous snake.

Seven metres of thick green and black scaly skin was heading straight for Eden. Its tongue flickered in the water as it followed the scent of her blood. Eden slowly edged away from the serpent.

Dylan outstretched his hand and thrust Eden onto the sideboard. She clung to him, and then further panic set in.

"Where is Niamh? Oh my God where is Niamh?" Eden instinctively began to get back into the water to find her friend, but was pulled back by Dylan.

"Stop," he said through gritted teeth. "You are going nowhere."

"Can anyone see her? Where is she?" Eden's voice began to take on a hysterical tone. Eden eyed the snake. She predicted that she had just enough time to sink quietly under the water and look for Niamh. Her heart thumped in her chest. She pushed Dylan's arm away and, before he could react, she took a deep breath and slipped under the green murky liquid.

The ocean was pouring in fast. Eden swam down and searched frantically amongst the debris; a long, thin shadow passed overhead. There was no sign of Niamh.

Eden was running out of breath.

She felt something grab her from behind and turned to see Oregan's face under the water looking at her. Oregan's blonde hair danced with the motion of the water, but it was her eyes that caught Eden's attention. Despite the decreased visibility, Eden could see Oregan's eyes were strange, almost reptilian. Her black pupils were no longer circular in shape, they had morphed into slits. She held Eden under the water, completely immersed. Eden struggled to get away, but Oregan was too strong. Eden looked into Oregan's face. Was she trying to drown her, or was she trying to silence her, so that the snake didn't detect their vibrations? Either way, Eden couldn't hold her breath any longer. She wasn't staying around to find out. She pulled herself from Oregan's cold, bony grasp and swam to the surface.

"Dylan, get me out of here," Eden sputtered as his arms locked around her.

Dylan dragged her from the water, and hoisted her up onto the table next to him. "What the hell happened down there?"

Eden tried to find the words but she struggled to understand it herself. Eden evaded the question. For now she would keep the unsettling, curious episode between her and Oregan.

"We need to move, now." Scotty interrupted. "God knows what else is swimming around in here, the boat is definitely going down. Our best bet is to try and swim back to those big black rocks we passed a while back, and then pray that we are found. I seriously can't deal with any more aquatic visitors." Scotty looked at the others for a response.

"You won't make it," the gravelly voice spoke again. Oregan remained in the water, her black T-shirt was drenched and clung to her body. She made no effort to climb out and join the others, she didn't cry or scream. She just stood there.

"Those rocks weren't far, why the hell not? We have to do something." Scotty looked at her in disgust.

"The rocks aren't far at all, but you can't swim to them, *you* don't know what is in the water." Oregan's eyes narrowed.

"And *you* do I suppose? How is it that you know so much Oregan? It seems to me that the rest of us are all fumbling around in the sodding dark, and then there is *you*, Oregan. Quite frankly, you seem a little too at home amongst this freakishness." Scotty was furious. He clenched his teeth together as he spat the words at the stranger. "What the hell is going on? Where is Niamh? Where is Riley? And what is doing this?"

"Scotty, if you listen to me, you may all just stay alive."

The group exchanged glances. Nobody was sure how to proceed.

"So what do we do, Oregan?" Eden was the most unlikely candidate to extend an olive branch to Oregan, but Eden was a pragmatist, her survival overruled the element of doubt. Perhaps Oregan was not to be trusted, but they had no other options.

"The upper deck is bound to be much dryer than it is in here. There is barely any water coming in at that level. We need to swim out of here, climb up the ladder, and congregate on the upper deck. I have checked the route and there is some wreckage around the hatch. Some broken pieces of wood are wedged in the gap, so we will need to swim under the water, as close to the ground as possible and squeeze through the gap. Once we are out the other side we can climb the ladder to the deck and wait to be rescued."

"I vote we do what she says." Amira's whole body shook as she spoke.

"Agreed," Eden echoed.

Dylan looked at Scotty. "Sorry mate, I think we should do what she says too."

"Fine. Well, clearly no one else can see that she has

developed a tinsy bit of a Medusa vibe since it all went a little *Anaconda* in here. But, fine, let's all go get killed. I'm totally on board with that." Scotty's sarcasm was biting. "But I must insist. Oregan, you first."

Oregan didn't hesitate; she disappeared under the water in an instant.

"See you on the other side." Amira went to take a deep breath but Scotty held her back.

"I don't think so. I am not being left here with these two, feeling like a right gooseberry." Scotty winked at Amira, he took a deep breath and plunged into the water with clear technique. Scotty had competed for the County in the national swimming gala.

Amira looked at Dylan a little bewildered.

"He has never been great at showing his feelings. Translated from Scotty language, what he actually meant to say, was that he wanted to check there was a safe passage, before letting you take the plunge."

Amira's cheeks coloured. She was genuinely touched by Scotty's chivalry, no matter how clandestine. She quickly followed suit with a lot more splashing.

Dylan looked at Eden and held her gaze for a long moment. "If you think I am leaving you in here alone then you really are losing it. You first, Miss Hollow."

Eden smiled. She took a deep breath and, without saying a word, flipped into the water. Dylan stood alone. Unlike Scotty, who was naturally gifted at just about everything, Dylan was not an accomplished swimmer. In fact, he struggled to hold his breath under water in the bath. Regardless, he knew he had to do this. He breathed deeply and plunged into the water. He swam down to the bottom and used his hands to guide his way along the floor. Despite the salty stinging sensation, he forced his eyes to remain open, so that he could negotiate the rubble blocking the doorway. He had almost cleared the passage when a long, dark shadow, with a triangular-shaped head was suddenly upon him.

Dylan's heart jumped into his mouth as the gargantuan

snake glided past him, its belly so fat he couldn't imagine what it had for its last meal. Dylan stopped dead in his tracks to let it swim by. As a child he had always been fascinated by reptiles, his father had brought him a small Hognose Snake, which he kept for a few years before it escaped from its vivarium. His mother had not been pleased. Dylan knew that despite appearances, snakes weren't vicious creatures and attacked only when they were hungry or to defend themselves. This snake had clearly had a meal, so it should continue on its path.

Dylan watched as the snake gracefully weaved in and out of the furniture. Suddenly, for no apparent reason, the snake began to change course. It turned to face him and recoiled its neck. Then, in one motion, it struck him, piercing his neck and releasing its venom. It only took a fraction of a second for the poison to enter Dylan's bloodstream. Instinctively Dylan opened his mouth to gasp for air, it was an involuntary reflex, water began to stream into his lungs. He couldn't believe what was happening. Images of his mother, his father, of Beth, Scotty and of course, of Eden, flashed through his mind, as he started to drown. Just as he began to lose consciousness, small hands grabbed his shoulders. The last thing he saw were her green eyes, then nothing.

Eden dragged Dylan's limp body onto the deck. Scotty dropped down to his knees and put his ear to Dylan's chest to listen for a heartbeat.

"He's still breathing." Scotty noticed the wound on his neck had already swollen and turned black, it looked like putrid, diseased flesh, he closed his eyes for a moment and tried to keep his composure. Panic surged within him.

"I trapped it in the cabin. I am pretty sure it can't get loose," Eden spluttered through tears, she held Dylan's head on her lap and mopped his brow with her jacket.

Scotty knelt down next to Eden. "We need to get help, like right now," he said, only to Eden. No-one else mattered in this decision, they would both put Dylan's life before

132

their own, and together they would make the best decision.

Eden nodded.

"I will go. I will be quicker on my own," Scotty said decidedly. "Whilst you were down there we found an inflatable lifeboat, I will use that and go and get help. The shoreline isn't far."

"Take Dylan with you. He will have better odds if he finds a hospital now."

"He won't make the journey," Oregan said absentmindedly. She stood just inches away listening to their conversation. "And they won't be able to administer an antidote without identifying the snake. They will have to come and get us first anyway."

"I'm not leaving him." Scotty's anger swelled inside him. He gestured to Eden to join him at the side of the boat, away from Oregan's prying. "I don't trust her and don't want her to be involved in this. The last time we listened to her, Dylan paid the price."

"I know, but annoyingly she's right. There is only room for two people, and you will be quicker and safer if you go with someone who can help you row. The weather is going to make it dangerous enough for the able-bodied. If anything goes wrong and you get blown into the water, which is a very real possibility, Dylan won't be able to swim to safety. I will take care of him until you come back. I promise."

"I will go with you, Scotty," Amira said sheepishly as she walked over to them. Scotty was deeply conflicted.

Their decision was interrupted by a strange slurping noise which came from behind them.

Eden's eyes opened wide. She couldn't believe what she was seeing. Scotty turned to follow her eye line.

Oregan knelt at Dylan's side. Her body was bent over his and her mouth was pressed up against his neck. She looked as though she was drinking his blood.

Scotty exploded. He grabbed Oregan's arm and dragged her away from Dylan.

Eden quickly resumed her protective position at Dylan's

side.

"What the hell do you think you are doing?" Scotty's face was red, his hands shook.

"I was sucking the venom out." Oregan wiped Dylan's blood away from her mouth, she looked genuinely hurt.

Scotty processed the information and his face turned from disgust to sheer relief as his friend woke up.

Chapter Sixteen

Dylan opened his eyes to a scene of total chaos. Eden was sat by him. His neck throbbed, he felt dizzy. The boats gentle rocking from side-to-side accentuated his nausea. Sweat collected on his forehead. His friends appeared to be arguing.

"Oh, thank God." Eden hugged him and quickly loosened her grasp as she felt him flinch with pain.

Dylan looked at Scotty and thought he saw a tear form in his friends' eye.

"Thank you," Dylan said to Oregan, who smiled through her humiliation. "Please go, Scotty. It's my best chance."

"Fine. But I will kick your ass if you die before I get back!"

With that, begrudgingly, Scotty and Amira made their way to the boat and into the vast ocean. Land seemed a thousand miles away.

Dylan, Eden, and Oregan sat silently on deck for almost an hour. Finally Oregan announced that she was going to check the snake was secure. As Oregan stood up and made her way down to the cabin, Dylan felt a pang of guilt. On the one hand, Oregan's behaviour had been extremely suspect since they set sail. Dylan knew that Oregan clearly had much more insight into the situation than she was prepared to discuss. On the other, as far as he could see, all Oregan had ever tried to do was help. She had probably saved his life, but had been made to feel like an isolated freak. He was too exhausted to explore the situation any further. He lay back on the deck and looked up at the starless sky - it was so still.

"I thought I was a gonner for a little while there."

"I did, too. How does it feel to be saved by girls?" Eden smiled.

"Hey, I saved you first," he laughed and turned on his side to look at her, pain shot through his neck.

"I suppose you did." They both went quiet and held each other's gaze. Eden looked away.

"What is it?" Dylan asked, he felt they had a newfound intimacy. He wanted to be honest and frank with her.

"What do you mean? What is it?"

"What is the secret? What really happened the night you left, all that time ago?"

"Dylan please don't ask me that. I want to tell you, but not yet."

"Well we might not get another chance." Dylan gestured to the incoming water.

"Why do you want to know so much?"

"Because it is the thing that is keeping you from me." He had finally said it. A load had been lifted. It was truly emancipating.

Eden paused, his words hung in the air. She looked into his deep dark eyes and lost herself for a moment. "That is *all* that is keeping me from you. You do know that, don't you?" Their faces were close. She couldn't stop herself from raising a hand to his cheek, his skin was soft but his stubble prickled her fingertips. She was so happy in that moment, but it was as far as she could go.

The mood was abruptly broken as an Adidas rucksack dropped down next to them with a thud. They both looked up.

"NIAMH!" Eden screeched and jumped to her feet. She lunged at her friend and held her tightly in a bear hug.

"We thought we had lost you. Thank God you are okay."

Niamh was dripping wet. There was a deep gash on her forehead, blood dribbled down into her eye. Eden wiped it away.

"I nearly wasn't. I got thrown during the crash, or whatever that was, and hit my head. I was spark out until

Oregan found me."

"Where is Oregan?" Dylan asked as he glanced around.

"She's just coming. We need to search this place and look for any dry mobiles, electronic devices, flares, anything that can send a distress signal." Niamh's sailing experience made her a useful person in an emergency. "C'mon, C'mon. We haven't got all day." Niamh slid the rucksack along the floor towards Eden who recognised the bag as Dylan's and began to rummage through. Finding the letter from her grandmother seemed almost a world away now. Eden plucked out a mobile and handed it to Dylan.

"It's dead," Dylan said, tossing it behind them.

Eden continued to sort through the contents. Something shiny caught her eye. "What is this?" She held the strange silver object in her hands. It looked like an antique Victorian hair comb, it was adorned with pearls, and had a strange spike protruding from one side. Eden wasn't sure if it was a vintage ladies accessory, or an instrument of torture.

"It was with your grandmother's letter, I figured it was your mothers."

At that moment Oregan arrived on deck. She was breathing heavily as she sprinted towards them, she was shouting something that Eden couldn't quite register.

"NOOOOOO! STOP, EDEN!"

But it was too late. The damage had been done.

Eden's hands began to shake uncontrollably, the peculiar artefact fell to the floor and the convulsions began. A sharp agonising pain sliced through Eden's body. It began in her head, it felt as though a needle was being inserted through her crown and into her brain.

Eden screamed in agony and clutched her ears to try and stop the deafening ringing sound, but it was no use, the pain was unforgiving, it travelled down her spine, slowly, vertebrae by vertebrae, until it was in her stomach. Eden doubled over and contorted into a tiny ball on the floor.

Kneeling calmly by Eden's side, Oregan picked up a sea drenched towel and began using it as a compress. Oregan's hand was steady, she didn't waver, not even for a moment, as Eden's jaws clamped together so tightly her teeth made a grating sound.

Dylan tried desperately to help, but there was nothing to be done. He heard a crack, and looked on in horror as Eden's legs snapped and bent forwards at the knee.

Her ankles turned outwards.

Another crack.

A small piece of bone splintered through her heel. She wailed in pain.

The skin was so tight it felt like it was on fire, as it stretched over her extended skeleton, it slit in places and blood began to drip from the wounds. The areas that weren't bleeding had turned dry and scaly.

Her jeans ripped at the seams as two fins pierced through flesh.

Then, finally it was over.

Eden lay there debilitated. She looked down in horror and saw that her legs had completely transformed into a burnt orange fishes tail. She looked from her body, which was so repulsive to her, to Dylan's eyes.

Eden would never forget the look on his face.

Chapter Seventeen

So, it was done. Eden had finally become Syren and fulfilled her fate. *It* had single-handedly delivered Eden back to them. *It* would be rewarded for this, they couldn't possibly overlook the good work that had been done this time, the 'chum' *It* had brought them. No, now they would have to take notice, finally *It* would be taken seriously. Eden had been missing for nearly seventeen years. To look at her now, no one would ever believe the power she possessed. Eden looked so fragile, so puny and pathetic, she doesn't know how important she is, how integral to their plan she will be. It was a shame about Dylan. *It* had grown to like him but he knew too much and was practically gift wrapped for them. He would be missed, but it was for a greater good. In a way, it was just like his sister Beth. He was a casualty of war, a martyr, giving his life for their breed. In the next life he would be richly rewarded.

Chapter Eighteen

Eden was trapped in her rancid body. She had the strongest sensation to throw herself into the sea, sink below the waves, never to return. She didn't want this. She didn't want any of it. That much she knew. It needed to stop. How was this even possible? This was the stuff of legends, not real life. It must be that strange pearl comb that was in Dylan's bag. What had it done to her? Of course some things made more sense now. Her bouts of sickness were not triggered by Dylan, or some psychosomatic condition, they were brought on by the object Dylan carried in his bag. The closer she came to it the weaker she would become. That is why she collapsed at Holly Cottage - she got too close to it. It infected her. It made her change.

Eden had a ferocious thirst. It was as though her whole body had been desiccated, she was drained of all liquid. Her throat was so dry, every swallow felt as though tiny razors were grinding her tonsils. She fought the need to dive into the water, but it was her nature now, and the draw was so strong. Her whole body itched, even on the inside, and it felt as if thousands of stinging nettles were rubbing against sunburnt skin. Suddenly Dr Lister's prognosis of water intoxication seemed cruelly ironic. In many ways it made sense to Eden, that in her human form her body would prepare for the transformation by storing water, but now that she had completed the change, every cell in her body screamed out for the sea. Her mind raced through so many things at once. *Was this it? Was she destined to be a freak forever? Could she turn back and resume her normal life? Or had the last few moments destroyed the hope of seeing her family and friends ever again? Were her aspirations for a future – a place at university, a career, a mortgage, a husband, a baby – entirely diminished, just like that?*

Eden couldn't bring herself to look at Dylan. She was terrified to move, fearing that if she shifted her tail, even a little bit, it would thrash about and flop around and she would want to die even more, the violation was just too much. It was better to bury her head in her hands, to block out everything and preserve the last remnants of her sanity. Between the cracks in her fingers, Eden caught a glimpse of Dylan's shadow; he seemed to be walking away from the whole nightmarish scene. But seconds later Eden felt his gentle breath against her neck, she looked up and there he was kneeling next to her and looking into her face. She knew he saw the devastation in her eyes, just like the child from years ago. Dylan gently moved loose strands of hair away from Eden's face, his hand travelled to the blistering scales, and he winced as he inspected the sores. He immediately stood up, removed his shirt, soaked it in sea water, and carefully placed it over her scales, as if she was made of glass. Dylan sat down in the pool of water, and placed his arm around her, kissing her hair as she rested on his shoulder.

"How long have you known?" He asked.

"I wasn't sure. I couldn't be certain until tonight. That night I had what my parents have since referred to as 'an episode'. I guess I experienced a fraction of what happened tonight, but it all stopped before, before…" Eden couldn't bear to say the words.

"Before *this* happened." He gestured to what lay under his sodden shirt.

"Yes, exactly. I have grown up with this hanging over me. I have always known there was something not quite right with me, I felt as though I was terminally ill or had some kind of disease that my parents couldn't bear to tell me about because of the shame. I guess this explains the whole water intoxication thing." Eden tried to smile but her cheeks couldn't quite manage it. "Maybe I am dying. I don't know anything anymore. I have no idea what I am." Her voice broke, she wiped away tears from her eyes. She felt his hand cover hers, as he slowly drew it back away from her face, he looked into her eyes and wiped another tear from her cheek.

"This 'thing' that you said will keep you from me, will only do so if you let it. It has always been you, Eden." He pulled her hands into his chest and moved his face to hers. Their lips touched softly. He held her there for a long moment, a safe haven amongst all the carnage, the pain, the fear.

He was hers and she was his.

The moment of solitude was over. Suddenly they were both aware of Oregan and Niamh's eyes upon them.

"What is going on, Oregan? You need to start talking right now." Dylan's tenderness transformed to anger in an instant.

Eden stared at the ground. Her mind and body had already endured too much; it was time to let Dylan take over. She desperately needed water to soothe her burning scales, they were beginning to catch and bleed with every movement. Dylan's shirt was drying out fast, she scanned her surroundings for moisture, anything to abate the unbearable stinging sensation. Eden's jacket had become hooked on a piece of broken wood that lay just a few metres away, it looked soaking wet. If she could prize the jacket free it would cover the majority of her lower body and provide her with much needed hydration. In one quick motion Eden doubled over and snatched the garment. But as she did so, something odd caught her eye.

Dylan and Oregan were locked into a fierce debate. "Look, someone was in Eden's house with me the other night, someone saw me take the letters and that weird metal thing from her dad's safe. I had left you just moments before outside the Pearl River Café. You have been acting weirdly ever since we set sail. Are you seriously trying to tell me that this is all coincidence?"

Oregan didn't have time to answer before Niamh

intercepted.

"And don't forget that it was Oregan who stood so calmly in the water, whilst God knows what lurked below the surface, and it was also Oregan who bathed Eden in salt water when she..." Niamh struggled to find the words, 'changed.'

Oregan shot Niamh a ferocious look.

"Don't trust her, Dylan. She's poison. She's lying. It was her all along. I am here to protect Eden. Why do you think I came onto the boat? I have never even met Riley, why would I risk my life for him? Why did I save you?"

"What do you mean 'protect Eden?' Protect her from what? What the hell is going on?" Dylan was at breaking point.

"I have heard just about enough of this." Niamh stormed to the back of the boat.

The rain began to fall from the sky. Oregan searched the boat frantically. She picked up a broken plank of wood.

"Quickly. We don't have much time." Oregan spoke directly to Dylan. "We have to stop her, restrain her whilst we have the chance, otherwise we are all as good as dead." Oregan's face was grave.

Dylan didn't move from Eden's side. "What are you going to do with that?" Dylan pointed to the plank of wood that Oregan held tightly with both hands.

"I haven't got time for this." Oregan turned to follow Niamh, wielding the wood like a baseball bat.

Eden couldn't bear to watch as the argument ensued. It was as though she was in a trance, as if her mind had mentally shut off from the rest of the world. She watched hypnotically as small droplets of blood from her jacket fused with the surrounding water. Eden drew the jacket closer and inspected the inside lining.

Eden shuddered as if someone walked over her grave.

The realisation hit her. She knew exactly who the killer was, and who was responsible for all of this. She looked up to warn Dylan.

Dylan grabbed Oregan. "STOP!" He pulled her towards him. "You can't do this."

Oregan raged away from him. He grabbed her again but Oregan's feet went from beneath her. The surface was covered in seaweed. As Oregan fell she smashed her head into a piece of protruding wood from the wreckage.

Eden screamed.

"Oh my God." Dylan tried to revive Oregan to no avail. After a few moments he sank down to the floor next to Eden.

"How did Niamh know that Oregan stood so calmly in the water?" Eden whispered. "She wasn't even in the same room. She wasn't even conscious. Unless she *was* in there with us. Oh God, Dylan, what have we done?" Eden saw a dark shadow appear behind Dylan.

In one slick motion, Niamh flung herself out of the boat and into the water. She was totally immersed. They watched in shock as Niamh's legs took the shape of a huge serpent. Green and black diamonds slithered under the water. Oregan was telling the truth.

Niamh was the serpent and she wasn't alone.

Eden and Dylan looked out to the surrounding water and saw the reflection of the moon shining into dozens of pairs of eyes.

Like stealth crocodiles they waited.

Dylan reached for Eden's hand as the Syrens opened their mouths, a deafening noise pulsed through the ocean. Dylan clutched his ears and doubled over in agony and, just like that, Eden was alone again. Eden's whole body shook, she grabbed Dylan and pulled him towards her. For the second time that evening she checked his pulse.

He was still breathing.

Chapter Nineteen

Amira looked up at the moon as the rain splashed her face and mingled with her tears. Salt water dripped into her mouth.

Scotty drew back his exhausted arms and rowed the boat around a large black rock that protruded out of the water. His muscles felt as though they had disintegrated and jelly was all that remained. Every move was agony, it took all the energy he could muster to stop his face from wincing. He watched Amira. Under her chunky black hood, her cinnamon eyes looked longingly out to sea. Her coat flapped around her shoulders, and her dark hair danced around her face as it caught in the wind. Scotty thought she looked like an imperilled heroine from a gothic fairy tale.

"I keep thinking that I will see him. That he will be sat around, with his feet up on a fancy yacht somewhere, wearing the most expensive designer sailing outfit money can buy."

"That does sound like Riley." Scotty smiled.

"You know all that pretentious stuff, it's just an act. He might appear confident and even a little arrogant, but there is a whole other side to him. When it's just us, he drops the act, and he is genuinely kind, he looks after me. He has been the most consistent person in my life. He really is the only boy to look beyond all of my window dressing, and actually see me."

"He's not the only one who sees you Amira," Scotty said, surprised by his own words. "So how long have you been in love with him?

Amira let out a quiet laugh. "He's like my brother! Anyway it really doesn't matter how I feel. Haven't you figured it out yet? Riley would be more interested in *you* than me."

Scotty blushed. He had never been good at reading people. "Sorry I didn't realise."

"I don't think anyone has been formally notified." Amira's sarcasm sounded harsher than she had intended. "It's just that Riley is a very private person. Things have got a lot better, but it hasn't been easy for him, growing up in a small town, managing his parent's expectations. There's not exactly a thriving 'scene' in Skull." She tucked a rogue lock of hair behind her ear. "But in the short time we have been at Cantillon, I have seen a real change in him. He seems so much happier, and settled in himself. And then this happened. We need to find him Scotty, there is so much he wants to do. This can't be it for him." Amira's face disappeared into her hands, her desperation was too much.

Scotty searched for some words of reassurance, but there was nothing he could say. Silence prevailed once again.

Eden stared at the slimy creature that used to be her roommate. She began to realise that all the disjointed pieces were part of a greater whole. In that moment she had clarity. The awful truth that had tapped away at her brain for the last few days was finally revealed.

Of course it was Niamh.

Niamh was integral to the sequence of events that brought the six of them to the boat tonight.

It was Niamh who followed her to the beach and tried to kill her in the Banshee's Burrow. Niamh's ability to shape shift into a snake would certainly account for the attack under water and the putrid stench she smelt that night.

Niamh had plenty of time, after failing to overpower Eden, to slip away and turn her attentions to Nancy. Apart from Eden, Niamh was the only one to have met Nancy, as they were both in John Fisher. She could have befriended her during the Carnival Noir and learnt that she had planned to leave Cantillon alone.

And then there was Riley.

The whole reason the six of them were on the boat in such perilous circumstances was due to the so-called information that Niamh had received from the sword swallowers. Eden now realised that there never was a private vessel, and that Riley, like Nancy and the numerous others before them, was, in all likelihood, dead.

Niamh's plan had nearly worked. She would have continued to go undetected if it wasn't for the small detail of the blood stain on Eden's shoulder. Eden had managed to injure her attacker the night of the Banshee's Burrow. Eden had pushed them away in the dark and they had screamed out in pain. The blood from the wound must have seeped into the attacker's jacket and then dried over time. So, when Eden borrowed Niamh's jacket earlier in the evening and got it wet, the old blood stain transferred to Eden's shoulder and she knew that Niamh had to be the killer. This was too much for Eden to process, she felt as though her head was about to explode.

"It's no good, you know. He will be out for hours." The familiar Irish accent came from behind her. Eden couldn't bear to look. Eden lifted Dylan's head and slid underneath him so his cheek was resting on her lap, his long eyelashes made his face look gentle and kind. Fury raged within her. Eden watched as the snake crossed over Dylan's body.

"Get off him!" Eden was incensed she grabbed the snake and flung it as far as she could. She didn't know where the strength came from but the slippery beast went hurtling across the boat and slammed into the side with a thundering crash. Niamh adjusted herself.

"You might want to be nicer to me. Your position is somewhat precarious."

Eden looked into Niamh's face, the face that had calmed her, laughed with her, even cried with her. Since arriving in Skull, Niamh had watched over Eden and cared for her like a sister. Now all that remained was a trace, a glimmer of recognition, a sense of déjà vu. The friend she had cared so much for, one of the few people who had provided her with a sense of belonging when she had felt at her most isolated, had disintegrated before her eyes. A cruel and malignant serpent was all that remained.

The creature closed its eyes, its snake-like tail became visibly fatter and longer, the weight gradually began to sink the boat. Eden looked at Dylan as the ocean spilled in around him.

"STOP! Please, stop. Okay, okay you have my attention. I will listen."

The creature opened its eyes, and the boat immediately floated back to the surface.

"I am not your enemy Eden, I am your friend, in fact I am family."

Eden shuddered at the thought.

"You are Syren, Eden. What that means won't be clear right now, but in time you can learn all about yourself, about us, and our kind. You will have to get into the water soon. You must feel it, that need. You will die eventually you know."

Eden looked down, her scales were even more cracked and bloody. Bits of them were flaking onto the ground. Her breathing was slow but she couldn't succumb. Not yet.

"I can tell you everything you need to know. I can help you to master the change, to transform without pain. I can teach you so much Eden. There is so much we can do together. You have a very particular purpose in our world. You are special Eden. Integral to everything. Come with me, discover it all."

Eden looked out to the water, she wanted it so much. "Why did you kill them? They were innocent, what purpose did it serve?"

"You don't know the first thing about it."

"Then tell me, because right now what possible reason do I have to go with you. You are a killer, a cruel hearted killer."

"It's all very basic, really. It is a matter of survival, the reason most people kill when you think about it. That and greed, of course. We need to go on undetected, so we have evolved over the years. I graduated as a Walker, a Syren that has ground legs, who has mastered the change. It's a very privileged position, there are very few of us you know. Walkers bring gifts back to the breed. That's what Nancy was – a gift."

"And Riley?" Eden's eyes filled up.

The creature's black vacant eyes looked back at her. They narrowed as it replied. "I never did like him. He was always so critical and so very lazy."

Eden had allowed herself to hold on to a tiny glimmer of hope that perhaps she had been mistaken, and that Riley was still out there somewhere. But now the last dregs of anything positive were draining away. "But why do you humiliate them? Why do you violate their bodies by dismembering them?"

The creature looked at her blankly. "Oh. I see. The severing of their limbs. That's not removed after death I'm afraid. It's very much pre-mortem. It's colloquially called 'chumming', these days anyway. Walkers track their prey, then wound them so they bleed out into the water. The blood and the 'yummy hum', that is what we call the vibrations that the wounded prey makes, then attract the breed, or to be specific, the Surface Dwellers, who then pull them under and deliver them back to the rest of the breed."

Eden felt a wave of sickness upon her. She couldn't bear to think of her friend experiencing such as blood curdling demise.

"Live food is so much better."

Eden needed her to stop. How could Eden be part of this, how could *this* be her fate. She was disgusted. "And what did you have planned for me? Why did you attack me that night on the beach and try again at the hospital?"

"I was never trying to hurt you, Eden. I wanted to bring you back home. I had orders from the powers-that-be to return you, so that is what I was trying to do. If you remember, it was you that hurt me that night. And as for the episode in the morgue, that wasn't me I'm afraid.'

"Then who was it?"

149

"Right, as fun as this paint by numbers is, it's time."

Eden couldn't believe the choice she was faced with. She was terrified of entering the water, she couldn't imagine what monsters lurked in its murky depths. Every now and again she saw ripples under the surface which sent tingles down her spine. But she had to do something, she needed the water, she couldn't be found like this. She looked at Dylan, his handsome, chiselled features and those soft eyelashes. How could she let him go? The creature watched Eden's conflict with interest.

"There is nothing for you above the surface now. He won't love you, not like this. Not when he finds out. I can offer you real family. Your heritage, the source of blood that runs in your veins. I can offer you history."

"What do you mean, *when he finds out?*"

The creature smiled as she said the four letter word.

Eden felt as though she had been punched in the stomach. The world was, once again, turned on its head.

"B-E-T-H."

Eden couldn't bring herself to contemplate it. It was just too awful. Eden knew that something was not entirely right in the Blake household, but she couldn't pin-point the source. There was just an overwhelming feeling of bleakness that never used to be there. At first, Eden had put it down to the divorce, and the fact that she was an adult now, so experienced the intricacies of human relationships in a different way to that of a child. But the more she considered the possibility that something had happened to Dylan's sister, the more sense everything began to make. Eden thought of all the details from the past few days that were archived in her mind. There were only three rocking chairs on the veranda, not four, one for Dylan, one for Judy, and one for Enid. Judy's tears over Nancy and her unwavering maternal instincts for Eden were all actions of a mother who had been robbed of a daughter. Judy's words, "Beth would have loved to have seen you," played over in Eden's mind, and then the confirmation came.

"A fifteen-year-old local girl from Skull went missing in

December last year," Eden said aloud, remembering her phone call with Amira. She was in shock.

"Well done. You got there eventually. Dylan's refusal to give up on Beth after she disappeared at Christmas time last year must have confused you. Maybe he didn't trust you enough to tell you. Maybe he thought you might run off again. He still talks to her ghost when he's on his own you know." A cruel smile formed on its putrid mouth. "Shame really. She was such a pretty little thing." The creature snarled and licked its lips.

Chapter Twenty

Amira and Scotty's little white boat arrived at the mouth of a towering black sea cave. The rocks stretched and curled as they ascended into the grey clouds. Scotty and Amira felt a chill as they took in the panoramic view. The cave's colossal stature would have been quite magnificent if it had not been so terrifying.

The eerie stillness was violently interrupted by a crash which echoed throughout the cave. At first it sounded like a clap of thunder which ricocheted off the cavernous walls. Scotty gently laid down the oars. As he moved a little closer to Amira he noticed ripples appear from under the surface of the water. Something large was swimming just under their boat.

"What the hell was that?" Scotty and Amira jumped to their feet and instinctively took each other's hand. They frantically searched around them.

"There it is again." Amira pointed to the dark water and the foam the creature left in its wake.

"Jesus, it's under the boat. In shark movies they always go under the boat. And then the massive great white shark catapults the boat and its inhabitants into the water." Scotty grabbed Amira and pulled her into him.

They waited, holding their breath.

Silence.

Then the creature came up once again, slower this time. They could just make out white flesh as it approached the surface and submerged once again.

"Where the hell is it?" Amira was trembling now.

In the distance Scotty could just about make out another boat that was shining a huge searchlight in their direction. If they could just survive the next few minutes they would be rescued. Scotty began waving his arms in the air and shouting to attract attention. A loud crash hit the back of their boat and knocked him off balance. Scotty plummeted into the water.

Amira screamed as Scotty frantically splashed his way to the surface and span around in total panic. The creature came closer and closer to the surface, just inches from him.

Spluttering noises began. It wasn't a creature at all, it was very much human and struggling to get to the surface. A head emerged from the murky depths. Amira would recognise his short haircut anywhere.

It was Riley and he was alive.

Eden pulled herself up in a blind rage. She lunged towards the creature. At the same time a lightning bolt illuminated the sky.

Quicker than Eden could process, something flew at the creature and knocked it into the water with such force they didn't resurface for several seconds.

A shrill sound that was excruciating to hear shook everything around them. It was nauseating.

At first, Eden couldn't make out what had attacked the creature. There was so much splashing as the ocean frothed and sprayed. It looked like a shark-feeding frenzy. She saw a dorsal fin emerge from the water and the ocean turned a deep shade of crimson.

Eden looked to where Oregan had been lying and saw only a pool of blood. And then her eyes couldn't believe what they were seeing.

A magnificent, colossal shark was swimming in the Celtic sea. Oregan was completely changed. In her shark-form she had tenacious strength and agility, she held the creature between her jaws and bit down, tearing a chunk out of the serpent's tail. Blood seeped into the ocean, as a huge gaping wound was exposed.

The creature was in agony and squealed in pain, it hissed at Oregan and recoiled its neck as if it was going to strike. Oregan was stronger and more powerful and had already bitten off a second chunk. The creature's tail was nothing more than a bloody stump, it squealed and sunk below the waves.

Oregan's body transformed back to its human form, but her tail remained. As she turned to look at Eden she saw terror in her eyes.

"I'm not going to hurt you, Eden. You are safe with me. I was sent to look after you."

Eden owed Oregan her life. "It was you that took me to the morgue and showed me Nancy's body, wasn't it?"

"Yes, I am afraid it was. I'm sorry about the photograph on the wall, but I didn't know what else to do. I wanted to warn you, to scare you, to make you run home to your parents. I have known about Niamh since she arrived. That's why I went with Amira to the Carnival earlier tonight. I was waiting for Niamh to take her next victim. I have been watching you and your friends since the first day of college."

Eden thought back to her arrival at Crookhaven Halls and the strange creature she glimpsed from her dormitory window. It wasn't a shark with a human body within its jaws; it was a shark-human Syren. *It must have been Oregan*.

"And your relationship with Dylan, was that all part of the act? Was that protection?"

Oregan's eyes looked down into the sea.

"No, that was all real, I'm afraid. Although I guess it's hard to tell how real, at least on his behalf."

Eden's eyes narrowed in confusion.

"You see, that's the blessing and the curse of our kind. Syrens have various abilities. For instance, we can shape-shift. We spend most of our time as Syrens, half human and half fish, but we also have other forms, too. Obviously we can change into human form but, as you saw from Niamh's transformation into a serpent earlier, and when I changed into a shark, each of us also has another form we can adopt in addition to our fish tail. It's kinda like our warrior self.

When we sense trouble, we turn and fight. When you get a little more used to shifting, we will discover what your warrior form is. But at the moment the change is so excruciating, in time it will get much more manageable, it should be seamless really. Oh, apart from the fact we leave a tiny trace of our change in the form of a gross second skin. You'll see yours when you move. It's like a snake shedding, except it's a bit more slimy and gloopy."

Eden remembered the foul substance floating in the sea the night she was attacked; it must have been Niamh's second skin as she changed into human form. A shudder ran through her.

"We also have other abilities. For instance, if we can get close enough to people we can affect their dreams."

"That would explain the nightmares I have been having. Not surprising, really, being tucked up next to a psychopath."

Oregan gave Eden a sympathetic smile. "And we also have the ability to lure men to the sea. You've heard the stories about beautiful mermaids singing enchanting songs to fisherman as they take them to their watery death? Well that's based on half-truths at least. Eden, we are beautiful and enticing and we have the ability to draw suitors, and to make them fall in love with us. So as far as Dylan goes, it's hard to tell how he felt about me."

Eden thought about her own relationship with Dylan. "So are you telling me that after all these years Dylan doesn't truly want me, but is actually under some kind of bewitching spell?" Eden's eyes filled up. She couldn't bear the thought of their connection being a lie.

"No, Eden, that's not what I am saying. You don't know how to channel your powers yet so of course what you have with Dylan is based on truth, at least for the most part. You have a shared history, a childhood together, all those things still count. But at the same time you need to realise that nothing is how it was. Everything you thought you knew is different. You have so much power within you, Eden, you just need to learn how to use it. Don't be afraid of it."

"What power? What do you mean? My whole life has been one huge mystery to me, I really can't deal with any more secrets, please just tell me. Tell me everything." Eden had never felt so vulnerable. She had to rely on a virtual stranger to tell her the truth about her life. But in that moment she didn't care if she sounded pathetic, or desperate, she needed answers.

"There is so much for you to learn about our kind. You have powers and control over elements that you cannot even imagine. Haven't you guessed it yet? Think about it, Eden. When you arrived on the beach the night of the attack, I'm guessing it was a calm and beautiful evening? But after the attack the heavens opened, and the stormy weather only subsided when you met Dylan. The night your parents took you away from Cantillon, didn't you say it was in the middle of a storm? And look at tonight. As you search for your friend, who you fear is dead, do you think it's a coincidence that we seem to be experiencing a perfect storm? None of this is a coincidence, Eden. Your love for the weather, those strange electrical currents that surrounded you on the storm chase, the fact that every time you are upset the sky turns black. Eden, *you* can control the weather."

Eden couldn't believe what she was hearing. She was still struggling to comprehend the fact that she wasn't even human, but controlling the weather? It was just so impossible.

"Syrens are oceanic creatures, Eden. The oceans control a huge variety of things in this world, including our climate and the weather. I told you, you are very special, Eden. If channelled properly, your gift, which you inherited from your mother, is potentially awe-inspiring. You have the ability to do so much good, but in the wrong hands..." Oregan's eyes closed tight.

"Go on," Eden said forcefully.

"All I ask is that you hear me out and just try to not hate me for what I am about to say."

"Please just tell me, Oregan."

156

"It started many years ago. There are two types of Syren, the Galodons, who are the oldest of our kind, and the Tidence. There was once a truly hateful Syren called Kalina Tidence. She was the cruellest of the Tidence breed and I'm telling you she had some serious competition. Anyway, the Tidence breed originally came from land, they have evolved from humankind, and because of this have much closer links to the climate. Some of them have the ability to cause a cloudy sky, a rain shower, but nothing like your ability. But unlike Galodons, they want to take back the land from the humans. You see, they've had a taste of it and now they want their share and more. For the Tidence breed, and particularly Kalina Tidence, who was the last remaining member of the original Tidence bloodline, life is all about power, about territory."

"Go on." Eden nodded.

Not unlike yourself, Kalina possessed powerful abilities. She could create precipitation. She was highly intelligent and the most beautiful Syren you could ever imagine. Kalina used both these attributes to lure the most powerful of the Galodon breed, and together they had a child. It was prophesied that their combined power would produce a first born daughter who would have the ability to change everything for Syrenkind. The child would have the ability to cause earthquakes, Tsunamis. Put simply, the child could take back the land. When Kalina fell pregnant, it was decided by the rest of the Galodons, that they would take the child and keep her away from her mother. So one night, on the very beach where you were attacked, the Galodon's watched Kalina give birth to a tiny daughter. As soon as she was born, they forcibly removed the child and left her with a human couple from the mainland, with nothing but a blanket and her mother's hair comb. Oregan paused. "Eden, that was sixteen years ago."

Eden closed her eyes as she took this in. "So I am the first born female to Kalina Tidence?"

"Yes. Ever since the night you were taken, the Tidence breed have been trying to bring you and your power back to the sea. That's what Niamh was trying to do."

"And where do you fit in to all this, Oregan?"

"Eden, the Galodon"s are the evolutionary breed of the Megalodon, the largest shark to ever swim in the sea."

"So you are..."

"Galodon." Oregan said the words that Eden couldn't. "Yes, I am part of the breed that took you from your mother, and denied you knowledge of our kind."

Eden didn't know what to do. Right now Oregan was all she had. Should she turn her back on the memory of her mother? A mother that she never knew? Eden's head was a mess. She needed time to process.

Oregan looked out across the water and saw a boat heading towards them.

"Amira and Scotty must have made it to the shore. I know this is so much to handle right now, but there isn't much time. Pick up the pearl hair comb you found in Dylan's bag and come into the water."

Eden looked at Oregan. She was utterly terrified.

"But what about Dylan?"

"He will be fine. He will wake up in a few hours with a bit of headache. But right now we need to get you back to your human form before that boat gets here."

Eden hated leaving Dylan, but being found like this was not an option. She stretched out her fingers and grasped the side of the boat, then, with all the strength she could muster, Eden dragged her wearisome body over the side and into the deep. As she met the water every part of her being sang out with pleasure. The icy cold water was rejuvenating, all fear and confusion ceased to exist, and with open eyes Eden swam down to the depths and let her nature take over. The water was so clear, the lights were lighter, and the darks were deeper. The fish swam alongside; they pecked at her skin, and swam in and out of her hair. In that moment they seemed to have an understanding. She didn't even need to take a breath. It was sheer exhilaration. This was where Eden was supposed to be.

A hand fixed on her arm. It was Oregan. She was

smiling. Oregan held Eden's hand and the two girls looked at each other under the water. Oregan put her hand to Eden's ear, gesturing to her to listen to what she was going to say.

"Blink if you can hear me, Eden."

Eden heard the words, but Oregan's mouth didn't move. Eden blinked.

"In time, we can help you to control your gift. But right now we need to protect you. I am going to use your mother's hair comb to make you change now, just as Niamh changed you earlier. Without the comb you cannot complete the transformation. That is why it must never get in the wrong hands again."

The realisation of Niamh's premeditated deceit hit home. Niamh must have been the one who broke in to Holly Cottage in search of the comb.

Eden blinked.

"As soon as you change you need to swim up and get into the boat. It's not safe down here for a human and you will lose your ability to breathe."

Eden blinked once again in response.

"I am going to stay down here for now, but we will meet again."

Regardless of what breed she was, Eden didn't want her to go.

"Are you ready?"

"*Blink*." Eden's eyes remained wide open, as she managed to communicate the word through her mind.

Oregan heard it perfectly. It confirmed that what she had heard about Eden was true. Eden could already communicate, something that took most Syrens years to master.

"Thank you for helping me, Oregan."

This time Oregan blinked.

Eden smiled.

"Now, brace yourself." Oregan took the pearl hair comb from Eden. "This is going to hurt."

THE END

Fantastic Books
Great Authors

CROOKED
CAT

Meet our authors and discover our exciting range:

- Gripping Thrillers
- Cosy Mysteries
- Romantic Chick-Lit
- Fascinating Historicals
- Exciting Fantasy
- Young Adult and Children's Adventures

Visit us at:
www.crookedcatpublishing.com

Join us on facebook:
www.facebook.com/crookedcatpublishing

Printed in Great Britain
by Amazon